nice and MEAN

Jessica Leader

ALADDIN MIX

NEW YORK   LONDON   TORONTO   SYDNEY

This book is a work of fiction. Any references to historical events,
real people, or real locales are used fictitiously. Other names, characters, places,
and incidents are the product of the author's imagination, and any resemblance
to actual events or locales or persons, living or dead, is entirely coincidental.

ALADDIN M!X
Simon & Schuster Children's Publishing Division
1230 Avenue of the Americas, New York, NY 10020
First Aladdin M!X edition June 2010
Copyright © 2010 by Jessica Leader
All rights reserved, including the right of reproduction
in whole or in part in any form.
ALADDIN is a trademark of Simon & Schuster, Inc., and related logo
is a registered trademark of Simon & Schuster, Inc.
ALADDIN M!X and related logo are registered trademarks
of Simon & Schuster, Inc.
For information about special discounts for bulk purchases,
please contact Simon & Schuster Special Sales at 1-866-506-1949
or business@simonandschuster.com.
The Simon & Schuster Speakers Bureau can bring authors to your live event.
For more information or to book an event contact
the Simon & Schuster Speakers Bureau at 1-866-248-3049
or visit our website at www.simonspeakers.com.
Designed by Mike Rosamilia
The text of this book was set in Garamond.
Manufactured in the United States of America/0410 OFF
2 4 6 8 10 9 7 5 3
Library of Congress Control Number 2009937536
ISBN 978-1-4169-9160-1
ISBN 978-1-4424-0669-8 (eBook)
1010 OFF

For Mom, Mandy, Tamar, and Adrien,
who make everything in life even better

❊ ACKNOWLEDGMENTS ❊

I am lucky to have had the insight and support of many wonderful people during the writing of *Nice and Mean*. I would like to thank the following ones especially:

Suma Chennubhotla, Lakshmi Kartha, and Sherrie Khadanga read the manuscript and showed me my characters in a new light. Similarly, Julia Morrison's expertise on video making taught me much more than where to indent.

My critique group, Darcy Cleaver Maloney, Jennifer McMaster, and Emily Wheeler, provided helpful feedback, kept me laughing at the Monkey House, and gave me a writing home in Louisville.

The community at the Vermont College MFA in Writing for Children and Young Adults taught me what it means to be a writer and supplied encouragement and laughs, especially when I should have been in bed. I am also grateful to my loving and supportive classmates, the Super-Secret Society of Quirk and Quill, and to Gwenda Bond and Varian Johnson, for their ever-ready guidance through the publication process.

My brilliant, generous, hilarious Vermont College advisers, Julie Larios, Rita Williams-Garcia, Tina Wynne-Jones, and Margaret Bechard, gave me one of the most important gifts of all: helping me tell my story. Margaret's direction on *Nice and Mean* in particular—tireless, thorough, tough, and reassuring—merits a great honking truckload of bonbons.

Great leaping and cheering thanks to my editor, Kate Angelella, for turning me into an author, sending me purple e-mails full of smart ideas, and generally making the entire process fun. Much gratitude also to my agent, Elizabeth Kaplan, whose insight on matters large and small steadies my hand as I go.

Thanks to my former students at West Side Collaborative in NYC and St. Francis in KY for being fun, smart, inspiring, and generally lovable. If my characters display one-third of your moxie (look it up), I will have succeeded in depicting middle-school life.

Two lifelong role models, Suzy Thompson and Joan Gardiner, have always encouraged me in my writing and graciously read many two-pound packages over the years when they had lots of other things to do. Thanks.

Amanda Leader, Jessica Green, Jessica Freireich, Susie Jakes, Tamar Paull, Maia Miller, Kate Lancaster, Julia Morrison, Susan Loucks, and Monica Flory—I am so proud to have you as friends. I often thought of you when I wondered what Sachi would do next.

My mother, Susan Leader, has always supported my dreams of writing, and for that I am truly grateful.

Thanks and love beyond all measure to my partner, Adrien-Alice Hansel, for her narrative genius, countless hours talking over the story, and unwavering understanding and support. As it turns out, Frances the Badger was sometimes wrong: Things *are* very good around here.

MARINA'S LITTLE BLACK BOOK,
Entry #1

* **Most Suspicious Behavior:** Rachel Winter
A tinfoil shirt, a popularity poll. What exactly is
Rachel up to?

* **Worst Mother:** Bianca Glass, a.k.a. Mom
Those pants? That attitude? This mother's
truly in a category by herself.

When I realized I was about to flip through the *Seventeen* Back-to-School Fashions for the third time that afternoon, I slammed the magazine shut and hurled it across the room. It flew through the air and landed against the garbage can with a big loud smack.

Exactly.

Where were my friends? Play practice ended at five. Even adding time for Rachel to do an extra shimmy, Elizabeth and

Addie to straighten chairs, and the three of them to snag snacks, they should've gotten here twenty minutes ago. And I should've been snacking with them, not sitting alone on my bed like someone who forgot to order a life.

I got up to grab my magazine, since my ninja throwing-moves had bent the cover. I couldn't believe how the play had turned into such a time suck. Elizabeth was the only one with a real part—did all of them really need to spend three afternoons a week in that sweaty drama basement? I had no desire to join the *Grease* cult—they'd already started quoting the songs so often that I'd had to tell them, "Hold the cheese, this is not Burger King." But if I'd known that my only company would be the blast of the AC and the thump of my iTunes, I wouldn't have blown off the audition so hard. How was I supposed to know that the lines in the play weren't the same as in the movie, or that they'd make us sing alone in front of everybody? Why hadn't anybody told me these things?

Ding-dong.

Took them long enough. I threw my magazine on the bed and ran down the hall to open the door.

"Marina, darling!" Rachel struck a pose in the doorway.

"Um . . . hey." I couldn't decide which was weirder—the drama-queen voice or her new getup. Today's silver shirt had already been a strange choice for a Wednesday, but now she had piled her long black curls on top of her head like she was about to walk a runway.

"Hey, Marina." Elizabeth gave me a hug, and I breathed in her sweet, flowery smell, which has been the same since second grade. When we first started having sleepovers, I used every soap and shampoo in her bathroom, trying to find that exact scent, but I never could.

We'd barely let go before Addie cried, "Reener!"—then strangled me and bonked me with her grocery bag. Four bottles of Diet Dr Pepper and one package of Mint Milanos straight to the shoulder blade.

"Ow!" I rubbed my back. "Hey, careful with the Pepper."

Rachel slipped into the apartment, laughing. "Nice one, Addie," she said.

Hunh? She and Addie were usually BFFs.

"Sorry!" Addie cried. She's half-Chinese, with freckles on her wide cheeks, and when they puff out, she reminds me of a sad puppy. "Are you okay?"

"I'm fine," I said as she stepped past me. "Seriously." It's too easy to make Addie feel bad. Even Rachel, her best friend, wanted to vote her Biggest Plebe in our online poll— "plebe" after the word for commoner—in social studies last year.

"Sorry we're late," Elizabeth said, following Addie inside.

"People kept fooling around while we were learning the dance, so Ms. Mancini kept us after five."

"Oh." I led them into the kitchen, the only place my mother would let us drink soda. "Were you late? I didn't notice."

"Well," said Rachel, "we were actually late for two reasons." She giggled.

As I hopped up onto the counter, the cold granite sent a shiver up my spine. I held out a hand and said, "Pepper me, Addie."

Her brown eyes gleaming, Addie handed one bottle to me, one to Rachel on the opposite counter, and one to Elizabeth at the breakfast table. "So?" Addie said to Rachel, once we had tapped down the fizz. "Are you going to tell her, or should we?"

Rachel grinned and squeezed her eyes shut, then blurted out, "I'm in love!"

Elizabeth and Addie cracked up.

"Again?" I untwisted my soda cap. Last year, Rachel had fallen in love about once a month.

"With . . . ," Elizabeth prompted.

Rachel and Addie answered together, "Julian Navarro!"

I choked on my soda. *I* was the one who had pointed out his hotness after summer vacay. Julian was mine.

"We're dance partners," Rachel explained, leaning so far forward, she looked like she was going to fall off the counter. "He kept messing up the hand jive, so I stayed after and helped him a little." She giggled. "He kept teasing me, like, 'Oh, prima ballerina thinks she's got moves,' but he totally liked it, I could tell." She drummed her feet on the cabinet below her. "He is so hot! Eee!"

"You guys looked like you were really into it." Elizabeth took a sip of Pepper.

"You're, like, *meant* to be together," Addie agreed.

I forced down a burp. Why was Rachel suddenly going after Julian? He was popular but also a homeboy, not like the artsy guys she usually went for. The clothes, the Addie slamming . . . what was going on with Rachel?

She'd come back different from camp, that was for sure—wanting to drag me to the boutiques listed in magazines, and suddenly obsessed with popularity. It had been her idea to poll our class for the "mosts"—Most Popular, Most Beautiful, Nicest Boy, Nicest Girl. I could tell she'd been upset when I'd won Most Popular, but please—did she not know how these things worked? I'd gone to elementary school with most of the kids at Jacobs, and she was still getting to know them.

Plus, she just wasn't Most Popular material. The other

day in math, when she'd cracked up over some weird thing, all the boys had looked at me like, *You're* her friend? She was fun—we'd spent all of last year trying to get revenge on Señora Blanca together—but fun did not equal popularity. Then again, if she could turn Addie into her own personal plebe, make Julian pay attention to her, and convince Elizabeth and Addie that she and Julian had potential . . .

I gulped my soda. The bubbles scraped against my throat.

Elizabeth already has a boyfriend this year—she's got that sort of nice-and-shy thing going on that the boys all love—but I hadn't gone out with anyone since last spring, and I would die if Rachel beat me to a boyfriend in seventh grade. Not that she could ever pull that off, of course. I totally had things that Rachel didn't. Like, I don't know, taste, or—

"Rachel, what are you doing?" I asked. She had hopped off the counter and started doing this weird dance, slapping her thighs and punching her own fists. Elizabeth and Addie were cheering her on.

"It's how he *dances!*" Rachel laughed. "Don't you remember the hand jive? From the movie?"

"Ah. Right." I twisted the Pepper cap as tight as it would go. I needed to put a stop to this Julian business before it turned into something big.

"That would be so funny if the two of you went out," I

Jessica Leader

said, sliding the Mint Milanos toward me as Rachel bopped away. "Do you think he likes tall girls this year?"

Rachel stopped mid-clap and looked down at her flats. "Maybe," she said, sliding into the chair next to Elizabeth. "I mean, whatever. We're just dancing partners."

I slit open the bag with my fingernail. I hadn't meant to make her all deflated, but she needed to find the map to the real world. For one thing, Julian was short. Julian's girlfriends had all been short. *I* was kind of short. And Rachel standing next to a guy made you think she was going to knock him over. I always thought that was one of the reasons the guys had steered clear of her last year, and hopefully, Julian would care about that too.

I pulled out the first cookie and bit. The mint tingled against the cherry from the soda, and I thought, *See. Marina knows what's good.*

"So, Marina." Elizabeth's voice broke into my thoughts. "You find out about Video soon, right?"

"Hunh? Oh, yeah." It was nice of her to ask—she *had* tied for Nicest Girl, after all—but I didn't care about Video the way they cared about the play. I mean, I could already make all the videos I wanted with my equipment at home. I had just acted like Video was woo because everyone had been squealing about getting into the play until my ears practically bled, and I'd needed something to come out of my mouth that wasn't barf.

"Ooh," said Rachel, "Video. With Mr. Tall, Dark, and Handsome." She wiggled her eyebrows, and I couldn't help laughing. Rachel's always had a crush on Mr. Phillips.

"I hope you get in," Elizabeth said. "That video you made for Angelica's birthday was so cute."

"Yeah," Addie agreed.

"Thanks," I said, and took a sip of Pepper. The video for my little sister *had* come out well. Even my dad had said so, during one of the three weeks a year he wasn't in Taiwan, or Thailand, or wherever it was that he always traveled for business.

"I remember when you were working on your video!" Rachel laughed. "We came to sleep over, and you were all like"—she hunched her shoulders and pretended to be staring at a computer screen—"'Don't bother me, guys, just a sec, just a sec.' Scary!" She laughed.

"Oh, like you didn't look weird when you were practicing for the dance?" I asked. "Hey," she said, "at least I wasn't talking to myself."

"What do you think you'll make your video about?" Elizabeth asked, gesturing with her chin for me to throw her the cookies.

Thank God for Elizabeth. I tossed her the Milanos bag and said, "Oh, it's a surprise."

Addie bounced in her chair. "Come on, tell us."

I raised my eyebrows mysteriously, my mind whirring like a D drive. I couldn't sit there empty-handed, not in front of the *Grease* gang. It would be fun to base my video on some kind of show. *Designer Threads*? Too complicated; no way did I want people sewing clothes. *Modelicious*? A cool idea, but you'd have to make a ton of episodes to show who had the most model potential. It *could* be fun to do something about our group, though. And if I could use it to make sure that Rachel would not be victorious in the next battle for Most Popular—

Wait a minute. *Victorious* . . .

"Okay, guys." I sighed. "I'll put you out of your misery. Here's my idea."

They leaned closer.

I smiled. *"Victim/Victorious."*

"Oh, nice!" Addie called.

"Sweet," Elizabeth agreed.

"Starring Jacobs kids as fashion victims?" Rachel asked. I nodded.

"I approve." She took a quick sip, then struck a pose. "And I will be your Most Victorious, I assume?"

I almost burst out laughing, because her silver shirt made

her look more like the biggest victim. But I grabbed my soda and forced on a serious expression as I guzzled and said, "Mmm-*hmm*."

"Uh, guys?" Elizabeth looked up from sliding apart her cookie. "Wouldn't that be kind of like the poll? I mean, do you really want to get in trouble again?"

Just then, I heard the sound of the key in the front door. Speaking of trouble. My least favorite voice in the world called, "Hello? Girls?"

"I'm in the kitchen," I yelled back. I don't know why she always calls "Girls." Did she honestly forget that my little sister lived at ballet and piano? Or did she want to make me feel bad that I was the only one home? Hey, I could dance if I wanted to. I'd just rather have a life.

The door swung open and I cringed. Why did my mom have to wear the orange pants on a day that my friends were over? They made her butt look like a pumpkin.

"Marina." My mother was frowning. "Your friends are here."

Behind my mother's back, Rachel mouthed the word *Duh.*

"Yeah?" I asked my mom. Nice to be polite to my friends! I always worried that Elizabeth left my house wanting to report my mom for cruelty to children. And sure enough, over my mother's shoulder, Elizabeth was glancing at me as if to say, *Should we go?*

I shook my head. If my mom was in a bad mood, I didn't want to be alone with her.

My mom set her shopping bags on the floor—bags I hoped were not full of pumpkin clothes. "I need to talk to you," she said.

"Can it wait until later?" I asked. Oh, great, she was mad at *me*! And Rachel—ugh—Rachel was widening her eyes at Addie like, *Ooh! Smackdown!*

"I'd rather deal with this now," said my mom, peeling off her leather jacket, "before your father comes home."

"We have lots of time before *that*," I said, thinking, *If he even comes home before bedtime.*

"That's okay." Elizabeth stood up and buttoned her sweater. "I need to get going, anyway."

Rachel hopped off the counter. "Me too," and Addie put in, "Me too."

I walked my friends to the elevator—so mad, I could barely see in front of me.

"Bye, Reener," said Elizabeth, giving me a squeeze. "Call me later, okay?"

"Thanks." I stood with my friends until the elevator came, then tried to sneak back into the apartment without my mom noticing me. No luck—she was right by the hall table going through the mail.

Except now she was totally obsessed with the bill in front of her, running a shiny, dark red nail down the list of charges and frowning so hard that lines appeared between her eyes. I started down the hall to my room, but she held up her hand as if to tell me to wait, so I rolled my eyes and leaned against the front door. She needed to make up her mind: yell at Marina or call MasterCard. And let me play on the Internet while she decided. What was the problem, anyway? I had gotten in trouble for the poll, but I'd finished my detention last week.

"I can't deal with these people," my mother muttered, tossing the bill aside. Then her gaze landed on me. "So, Marina," she said. "I got a call today about your vocabulary quiz."

"What?" I asked. "What about it?" Had I failed a quiz already? I had studied!

"Ms. Avery said you had the same answers as Rachel," my mother told me. "Is that true?"

"What?" I asked. "Oh my gosh, it's not like there are answers. You were supposed to write sentences that showed you knew the meaning of the words. Yeah, Rachel and I came up with the sentences together, but we each remembered them on our own. Rachel's not even in my class. Why does Ms. Avery even care, as long as the sentences are right? She just doesn't like me."

"Calm down, Marina." My mother closed her eyes and rubbed her forehead. "You don't need to go into hysterics about every little thing."

"I'm not going into hysterics," I told her. "I'm just saying, we didn't cheat."

"Nobody's accusing you of cheating," my mother said. "She just said you had the same sentences and wanted to figure out how that happened."

"Well, tell her what I told you," I said. "We studied."

My mom ripped into another envelope. "She'll probably want to hear it from you."

"What?" I had already spent more than enough quality time with my Head of House. "Can't you call her? She called you."

"Marina . . ." My mother tugged the letter out of its envelope. "I don't have time to go through ten rounds of phone tag with the teachers at your school. You see her every day. Just talk to her."

"Fine." I pushed myself off the door. "But if I end up in detention again because she doesn't believe me, you're going to have to talk to her, anyway."

"You know, Marina." My mother sighed. "I come home from a long day—"

Of spas and waxes, I thought.

"—and I don't think it's too much to ask that sometimes you're in a good mood."

"And I don't think it's too much to ask," I shot back, "that sometimes you're on my side."

I didn't want to hear what she said to that, so I stomped down the hall and slammed my door. Then I texted Rachel.

Ms. A called my mom 2 say we cheated
on vocab quiz. Hate her!

I watched the phone until a text from Rachel buzzed back:

Stnx 2 b u!

U 2, I wrote back. Did Rachel think Ms. Avery wouldn't call her parents?

The phone buzzed again with Rachel's reply:

My parents will be like pls, we dont care.

I snapped the phone shut. How could I have forgotten? Mr. and Mrs. Winter thought Rachel was so perfect, they'd probably get mad at Ms. Avery for calling them. But why did she have to be such a raging jerk about it? Elizabeth would have been nice. Addie would have said, *Poor Reener!* It was just Rachel who turned it into something to show off about.

I grabbed my Little Black Book off my bedside table and started scribbling. If winning was what Rachel wanted, I could think of plenty of poll categories for her to come in numero uno.

SACHI'S VIDEO NIGHTMARE #2.0

INTERIOR. JANE JACOBS MIDDLE SCHOOL LOBBY—DAY

Students crowd around a bulletin board.

CLOSE-UP: SACHI, her face alert.

CUT TO: the bulletin board. A piece of paper
reads, "After-School Activities."

CLOSE-UP: the word "Video" and a list of
names underneath it.

PAN down the list of names, resting on: SACHI
PARIKH.

Sachi claps her hands in delight.

    SACHI
    Yes! I made it! Oh, thank you,
    thank you, thank—

She knocks into someone and turns to see MR.
PHILLIPS, a teacher who has appeared as if from
nowhere wearing a black suit and dark glasses.

    MR. PHILLIPS
    Sachi Parikh?

```
SACHI
(gulps)
Yes?

MR. PHILLIPS
(briskly)
Come with me, please. We have some
questions about your permission
slip.

STUDENTS JEER and WHISPER, "Busted!"
```

"Excuse me," I said, weaving through the crowd outside of school. "Sorry. Pardon me."

"Hey, Sachi!" said a voice.

I turned to see Tessa, from my math class, disentangling herself from her friends. "Oh, hi!" I replied. I really wanted to get into the lobby, but I didn't want to be rude, so I asked, "How are you?"

"Good. Listen." She sighed. "I lost that pencil you lent me."

"Oh!" I felt bad that she felt bad. "That's okay."

"Are you sure?" Her dark skin wrinkled with worry. "It was one of those nice mechanical ones."

I tried to smile, but all I could think was *Video, Video, Video.* "It's okay," I told her, "really. Hey, I need to check over my homework, but I'll see you in math, okay?"

Her face relaxed. "Okay, thanks. Yeah, see you later."

I wove through some tiny sixth graders, careful not to shove into them but barely able to wait another second. We'd handed in the permission slips for after-school activities on Monday—they had to post the list today! When I came close enough to the door to give it a good yank, I burst into the lobby, looked toward the bulletin board and—

Oh. No list.

Not that I could read the bulletin board from all the way across the lobby, but last year, when my sister Priyanka had wanted to know whether she'd gotten the fun Test Prep teacher or the strict one, seventh and eighth graders had flocked to the board in such a mob that I'd had to wait on the edges until Priyanka had come back with the bad news. Some kids were milling around by the board today, but they looked more like people waiting than people who'd just found something out.

I walked over to my spot near the library, trying to stay hopeful. I *had* gotten to school pretty early. Maybe they'd put up the list before homeroom. After all, activities started next Tuesday, and today was Thursday. Surely they wouldn't wait until next week to tell us. My stomach clenched with the thought that I'd have to spend the whole weekend worrying whether I'd gotten into Video. The teachers wouldn't notice that the signature on my permission slip didn't really match the one on my sister's . . . would they?

"No way," said a giggly voice, "you didn't count that right."

"That's because I can't do it when you're moving!"

I looked up to see Flora and Lainey heading toward me. Lainey was clutching Flora's collar, and the two of them were laughing.

"Hi!" I laughed too because they looked so silly. "What's going on?"

Flora sank down next to me. "Not much."

I inched away to give her room, since the pin collection on her bag could scratch you if weren't careful.

"Hey." Lainey smiled as she sat on the other side of Flora, her dirty-blond hair pulled into a messy bun. "What's up?"

"What were you guys talking about?" I couldn't imagine why Lainey had been holding on to Flora's collar.

"Oh, nothing." Flora shook her head, but she had a little smirk that made me think it was actually something.

"Flora wants me to get her some of that bicycle-chain jewelry they sell near my house," Lainey explained, "you know, like my bracelet." She rooted among the many bracelets on her wrist and ran her finger over a thick silvery one that I now realized was a chain from a bicycle.

"Oh, right," I said. "I like that one." Honestly, I thought it was sort of strange, but I knew Lainey was proud of it.

"Thanks," said Lainey, pleased. "Anyway, you have to tell the people at the store how many links you want, so I was trying to measure with my fingers, except *somebody*"—she leaned into Flora, who let out a barking laugh—"kept moving, so I couldn't get it right."

"Oh, funny," I said. Although why was that such a big deal that Flora didn't want me to know about it? "You should let her count, Flora. That bracelet would look good on you."

"Hey," said Lainey, "do you want me to get you one?"

Flora burst out laughing. "Oh, yeah, right."

"What?" I asked, surprised.

Flora shook her head, chunks of dark brown hair falling from her ponytail. "No offense, Sachi, but I don't think you're the bicycle-chain type. I mean, the poll said you were a *Nice* Girl, not a Tough Girl."

"Ugh, do not even mention that stupid poll." Lainey scuffed her pink high-tops against the wall opposite us. "That thing was evil."

"Yeah." Flora snorted. "Weirdest Girl." She kept saying it like that, but I knew she liked her title.

"You'll be on it if they do it next year," I assured Lainey. "For Best Singer, maybe." She was new this year, so people didn't know her that well yet, but she was playing Rizzo in *Grease*, so she must have been good.

Lainey chipped at her purple nail polish. "I guess. But you're, like, the only nonpopular person who got something good. Not that those girls are popular with *me*, but you know."

I crossed one leg over the other. "Yeah . . ." I had to admit, at first I had been flattered to have made it onto the poll. But lately I had started to wonder, what did "nice" mean? That I lent so many people pencils, I had to dip into my tiny allowance to buy more? Or that I didn't say anything when Flora acted secretive about a necklace? "Nicest Girl" may have seemed like a compliment, but it was part of the reason I needed to get into Video.

SACHI'S VIDEO FANTASY #2.1

INTERIOR. JANE JACOBS AUDITORIUM—DAY

> LAINEY
> Sachi, your video was amazing! You
> may be Nicest Girl, but I'm going
> to call you Most Creative.

> SACHI
> (*modestly*)
> Oh, thank you.

FLORA
```
Lainey, Sachi has always been
creative. Don't you ever see her
stories in the hallway? She's more
than just the perfect score. Maybe
it's not obvious to you, but Sachi
and I have been best friends since
third grade, so I know these things.
```

I was so lost in my thoughts, I didn't notice when it happened, but a teacher must have posted the list on the bulletin board, because all of a sudden there was a stampede! Seventh and eighth graders mobbed the board in layers so thick, I couldn't even see the board itself.

"What *is* that?" Lainey asked.

"I think it's the after-school activities list," I responded, my heart thumping. I sat frozen between them, not sure if I should move. Of course I wanted to see if I'd gotten into Video, but I wasn't sure I wanted Flora and Lainey to be there when I did. What if the teachers noticed that the signature was funny, and had written "See me" next to my name?

Well—even if that was the case, I had to know. I jumped up and said, "I'm going to check out the list."

Flora squinted up at me. "Are you that excited about Test Prep?"

"Um . . . I also requested Video." The crowd was gathering more people by the second.

"No way!" Flora scrambled to her feet, and Lainey did the same as my heart squeezed in protest. "That's so cool. I thought your parents were making you take Test Prep. What did you say to them?"

"I just asked and they said yes," I replied, heading for the board. I wished she hadn't said that in front of Lainey. They were already getting close because of the play. What if Flora told her things about me that made me seem immature? "It wasn't a big deal."

Just then, a boy pushed past me and elbowed me, hard.

Ow! I rubbed my arm. Was that my punishment for lying? Because I hadn't only lied to my friends. I'd deceived my parents as well, only far, far worse.

SACHI'S VIDEO NIGHTMARE #2.2—A TRUE STORY

INTERIOR. SACHI'S PARENTS' BEDROOM—NIGHT

CLOSE-UP: a credit card, flipped over. A piece of scrap paper. A hand practicing a signature.

>SACHI'S MOTHER (*offscreen*)
>Sachi? Why aren't you in bed?

```
PAN from Sachi's hand to her face as she
gasps.

          SACHI
          Coming!

Using the signature she's been practicing,
Sachi scrawls her mother's name on the after-
school activities form.
```

I brushed the memory from my head. I just needed to find out whether I'd gotten in—then I'd deal with the consequences.

A space opened up in front of the board, and I darted into it. I found the words "Video Lab," scanned the end of the list for "Parikh," and—

"Yes!" I clapped. "I'm in!"

"Awesome," said Lainey. "What are you going to do it on? Can we guest-star?"

I laughed. "Oh, gosh, I don't know." I had thought about what I might do, and it didn't involve playing a part. But it could, possibly, so I said, "I mean, of course you can."

The first bell rang, sending a groan rippling through the lobby. "We should go," Flora said. The laughter I'd felt a moment ago dried up, because I remembered something else I had to worry about: Priyanka.

SACHI'S VIDEO NIGHTMARE #2.3

INTERIOR. JANE JACOBS MIDDLE SCHOOL LOBBY—DAY

Sachi's sister, PRIYANKA, enters the lobby
and makes a beeline for the list. She reads
it, and her eyes bulge out in shock.

>PRIYANKA
>(*turning to Sachi*)
>You're taking Video? What is your
>problem? I'm calling Ma!

>SACHI
>Priyanka—let me explain—

I had to intercept her before she saw the list.

"You guys go ahead," I told Flora and Lainey. "I need to
tell Priyanka something."

"Priyanka? Get me outta here!" Flora bounded toward
the stairs. Lainey ran after her, asking, "Why?"

Flora made no secret of finding my older sister cross and
dull, and though I wished she wouldn't be quite so obvious
about it, I couldn't blame her.

Make that cross, dull, and punctual, I thought, because, as
if on cue, Priyanka strode into the lobby, her hair frizzy
in the humidity, despite her braid. A crowd had gathered

again around the list, and she began striding toward it, but I blocked her path. "Hey!" I said, trying on a broad smile. "How are you? Did Pallavi get to school okay? I'm sorry she was so cranky on your morning. What do you think was bothering her?"

Priyanka wrinkled her nose, adjusting her glasses. "What's going on?"

I blinked. "With me? Nothing. Well, my backpack is kind of heavy, but—"

She rolled her eyes. "What do you want, Sachi?"

My heart sank. "What makes you think I want something?" In the old days, Priyanka and I always talked about our little sister. In fact, last year at this time, we were dropping her off at school together. But ever since the winter, Priyanka had gone from doing everything with me to criticizing everything I did. I had no idea what I had done to deserve it or how to make things right. Now, as she stood in front of me with her arms folded, her long braid flopping over her shoulder like the tail of an agitated raccoon, I thought, *She probably won't listen, but I have to try.*

"Okay," I said, taking a deep breath, "you know how I wanted to be in the after-school Video class?"

She shifted her jaw to the side. "Yes?"

"So I sort of . . . got in. And—"

"What?" She spoke with such force that the koala bear hanging from her backpack jumped on the end of its key chain. "What did you do, you forged the signature?"

I looked at the koala's matted fur, feeling like I was dangling from a chain myself. "Maybe."

As two girls walked by, one pointed at the koala, and the other one giggled. I felt my face grow hot.

"Ma and Papa are going to kill you," Priyanka declared. "Do you really think they're not going to find out? What do you think will happen when your class takes the practice test? They'll know you haven't been studying."

I cringed. Priyanka had gotten to the second part of my plan sooner than I had wanted her to. "Well," I said, "I was hoping you could lend me your books from last year."

She stared at me. "Are you crazy? I'm not helping you with this."

"Please?" I begged. "I'll make sure they don't find out."

"I can't even believe we're having this conversation," she said. "Why do you need to take Video *now*? Just do it next year, when you've already gotten into high school."

Would she understand my reasons if I explained them? I had to try. "Do you remember the video in last year's Arts Assembly?" I asked. "Where they talked about the different nationalities at school like we were countries on the news?

You know, when the white girl asked the Muslim girl in the head scarf for the ketchup, and the voice-over said, 'America recognized Pakistan today'?"

I thought it would make her smile—I knew she'd liked the video too—but she folded her arms. "You think because those two boys made a video and got into Stuyvesant, you will too?" she asked. "You know that it's just based on test scores, right?"

"Yes," I said impatiently. "I know how it works." How could I not, with my parents quoting from the *New York City Specialized High School Handbook* every evening? "I just meant—that video was so cool, and I want to make one like it. Not exactly like it, though—more like a sequel. If I wait until next year, people won't even remember the first one."

"So?" said Priyanka. "What's worse—people not remembering last year's video, or being the only cousin who didn't get into Stuyvesant? I mean, if *I* get in." Her tone showed that she thought she would.

"I know it doesn't seem like a big deal, but . . ." I didn't think I could tell her the other reason I had to take Video now—that I didn't want to go through Jacobs known just for my grades, or being Nicest Girl. The boys who had made the video last year—everyone was talking about them after the Arts Assembly. I wanted that to happen to me. "I really want to be in Video *now*."

Then I noticed that there were only two minutes left until homeroom—time to speed things up. "Look," I said, "if you keep it a secret, I'll let you have the computer first every day for a whole month."

"You think I'll lie to Ma and Papa just to use the computer?" She started walking toward the stairs, fast. "Ha."

I wanted to cry, but I had to keep going. "Okay," I said, struggling to keep up with her, "I wasn't going to say this, but if you tell Ma and Papa about Video, I'll tell them that when you went to the movies this summer, it wasn't just with the cousins."

She whirled around. "You wouldn't!"

I shrugged, trying to seem cool for once in my life.

"Fine," Priyanka said. "Take Video, see if I care. If you end up going to a bad high school, don't come crying to me about it."

I itched to crack my knuckles but restrained myself. "You won't tell them?"

She pursed her lips. "Fine. But you'd *better* use my books. If Ma and Papa find out you ditched Test Prep, I don't want them to blame *me* for letting *you* get a bad score."

"Fine."

Priyanka stepped up the stairs two at a time, which I recognized as the sign that we were done. I let her go for two paces, then scrambled on up. I didn't want to be late to homeroom on top of everything else.

But, I reminded myself as the air burned in my lungs, she had said yes. And that meant—*Video.*

MARINA'S LITTLE BLACK BOOK,
Entry #3

* Most Likely to Be Booted Out of Video by Marina Glass:
Everybody in the Video Lab
Who are you, and what have you done with the hotties?

* Most Likely to Become a Sleeping Pill: Mr. Phillips
Next time I have trouble falling asleep, I'll imagine
his voice and . . . zzz.

I pressed so hard against my Little Black Book that I dented
my lavender Pilot Precise Rolling Ball's extra-fine tip.

"Crap," I muttered, but nobody heard. They were all
too busy drooling over Mr. Phillips, leaning forward in
their desk chairs like he was giving out swag instead of
obvious rules about how to handle equipment. Like,
oh, wait, *don't* throw the video camera? Forget about Tall,
Dark, and Handsome—Mr. Phillips was Tall, Dark, and

Boring. And why was he shuffling through his papers again? He wasn't going to give us another handout, was he?

"So I decided," Mr. Phillips said, "that to simplify things, I would assign partners."

My pen tumbled onto the carpet.

As I dove down to pick it up, I thought, *partners*? How could he do that to us? He didn't even know us. And I knew—I just knew—that he would put me with the biggest squeegee in the room.

"Squeegees" were what my friends and I called nerds after the school counselor outlawed words like "geek," "dork," and "nerd." You could outlaw a word, but you couldn't outlaw a nerd, and the circle of kids in the video lab was proof. Exhibit A: a boy who looked like he'd chopped his bangs with safety scissors. Exhibit B: another boy who shot up his hand to answer questions before Mr. Phillips had even finished asking them. And Exhibit C: that Indian girl from homeroom who was actually taking *notes*.

How could there not be even one hot guy? Just one, to talk about while Rachel mooed over Julian and his arm-flinging technique—was that so much to ask? I'd thought video would be woo. Instead, it was poo.

Mr. Phillips sifted through the papers on his desk. I gripped my pen. Partner time.

"Eli and Trevon," said Mr. Phillips, reading from a list. "Ethan and Ricky. Makayla and Li-Ling . . ." *Just get to Marina,* I thought. After what seemed like forever, he finally read out: "And Marina and Sachi."

Sachi. Right. The one with the big smile and wrinkled tank top.

Terrific.

Mr. Phillips must have said something about sitting with your partners, because the next thing I knew, everybody was jumping up and dragging desks across the room. I didn't bother. She'd come over to me sooner or later.

"Uh, Marina?" said Sachi, once she'd plunked her chair next to mine. "I'm Sachi. I think we're partners?"

I slammed my Little Black Book shut. "I know."

Had Mr. Phillips said, "Now hover over your partner, clutching your giant spiral notebook like it's a squirmy kitty"? Nice to make an effort.

I tried a smile. She smiled back and slid into the seat next to me. Effort? Check.

"Should we do the partner questionnaire?" she asked, trying to smooth her hair. It was nice and thick, I'd give her that. Her big brown eyes were glittery too, if you could get past the hair frizz and the pointy chin.

"We *could* do the questionnaire," I said, as if I was

thinking it over, "but I actually really want to talk to you about my idea."

She drew back, and I thought, *Yep, this one wants to follow all the rules.* So I was surprised when she said, "Okay. What?"

I leaned in. "Here's what we should do: *Victim/Victorious.*"

I'd thought that Sachi would clap and squeal the way Addie had. Instead she started twisting this big gold ring around her left index finger like it was going to bring her back to Oz.

"*Victim/Victorians?*" she asked. "Is that historical fiction?"

"*Victorious,*" I corrected her. "On Channel 32? Thursdays at nine?"

Sachi's fingers traced the edge of the page. "We don't have cable."

"Oh." How did she live? "It's ragingly cool," I assured her. "They show stars on the red carpet at different events from the week, and then in the studio these two hosts, Esmé and Scotty G, rate them 'Hot, Hot, Hot!' or 'Not! Hot! At! All!'" I scanned her face for a sign, please God, that it rang a bell. But she still looked confused, so I asked, "Haven't you ever heard people say 'Not! Hot! At! All!'?"

"I think so," she said. "Maybe."

Oookay.

"Anyway," I went on, "I thought we could do a show about the fashion victims and, um, victors"—was that the right word?—"at Jacobs! You know, whose clothes are in and whose are out? Elizabeth Ellis can totally do the accent for Esmé, the host, and I know *tons* of people who'd play stars."

I sat back and tightened the belt of my new cream-colored wrap sweater. I'd saved it for the first day of this class—not that anybody was there to appreciate it—but at that moment it did sort of make me feel like a movie producer. "Cool, right?"

"That does sound fun," Sachi said. "And actually, I had an idea too."

I breathed out through my nose. Here it came—the squeegee pitch. I would listen to be polite, but I couldn't imagine anything better than *Victim/Victorious.*

"Okay," I said. "What's your idea?"

She bit her lip, then began talking quickly. "Doyou-rememberthatvideofromlastyear—aboutthelunchtables?"

"Ummm." I talked slowly, hoping it would calm her down. "Yes."

It seemed to work a little. "I thought maybe we could do something like that. Something where we interviewed people to see what they thought about different nationalities at Jacobs."

She didn't have much to say after that, and I could see that she didn't think her idea was so great after all. I didn't want her to feel bad, though, so I said, "Yeah, that video was kind of fun, but it's already been done, you know?"

"Yes," said Sachi, "but maybe we could pick up where they left off? Maybe we could ask people why there have been no Asian girls on the basketball team for the last three years. At least, they're not in the yearbooks. I don't think it's prejudice, so are Asian girls just not trying out? Something like that."

Squeegee alert! Mayday, mayday! "I know what you mean," I said, "but that does sound like the one from last year. You don't want people saying you're trying to *copy*."

"I wouldn't copy," Sachi said quickly. "I just thought—"

A deep voice nearby interrupted. "And how is this group doing?"

Sachi and I looked up to see Mr. Phillips standing over us.

"We finished discussing the questionnaire," I told him (lie), "so we were talking about the topic of our video." It was nice to tell a teacher what I'd gotten done, instead of being yelled at for "getting off task." Teachers have been writing that on my report cards since kindergarten.

"I see." He plunked down his stool and sat. "And what have you come up with?"

I told him, "We were thinking of doing *Victim/Victorious*."

"Hmm." He rested his chin in his hand, his fingers brushing against some little black curls that did not add up to a beard. "Is that a reality show?"

Did these people live under a rock? "Uh, no. More like a fashion show, but kind of like news. See, the stars walk down the red carpet, and the hosts, Scotty G and Esmé, like, rate the outfits, and—"

"I think I get it." He turned to Sachi. "Do you watch this show?"

Oh, so I didn't even get to finish my sentence?

"I haven't actually seen it," she admitted.

"But it's going to be really cool," I said, and told him how I had leftover red carpet at home from when we had our front hall redone.

"Hmm," he said when I was done. "You should have a look at it, Sachi, before you commit to the topic. It may be hard to do a parody of a show you've never seen."

A parrot? Who said anything about parrots?

"You don't have to decide on your topic until the next class," he said, "so why don't you think of a few other ideas you could work on?" He stood up and headed on to the group next to us.

I snapped my pen shut. If *Sachi* had come up with the

Victim/Victorious idea, he would have been like, "Oh, Sachi, you are a genius, let me have your autograph." Instead he was trying to make me feel like I had twisted her arm, when in reality her plan would put people to sleep. Did teachers talk about who they were going to like and who to be mean to? I lay my arms across my desk and rested my chin on my hands. I hated school. I just hated it.

Sachi glanced at Mr. Phillips, who was now hovering over another group, then flipped to a new page in her giant spiral. "Should we start making a list?"

A list of what—new ideas? *Victim/Victorious* was the one and only best idea. Plus, how else could I get in my little dig about Rachel's clothes? There was no way I would change my mind, but Mr. Phillips was looking at me from across the room, so I needed to play a little pretend.

"Go ahead," I told Sachi, but in no way did I mean it.

SACHI'S VIDEO NIGHTMARE #4.0

INTERIOR. JANE JACOBS MIDDLE SCHOOL
AUDITORIUM—DAY

CLOSE-UP: movie screen. The words
"VICTIM/VICTORIOUS, BROUGHT TO YOU BY
MARINA GLASS"

In very small letters: "and Sachi Parikh."

Students CLAP listlessly.

CUT TO: the audience.

CLOSE-UP on Sachi, with FLORA and LAINEY on
either side.

>	FLORA
>	That was . . . weird.
>
>	LAINEY
>	Hunh. I didn't know you liked
>	*Victim/Victorious* so much, Sachi.

CUT TO: Priyanka, standing at the end of
Sachi's aisle.

PRIYANKA
You made me lie to Ma and Papa for
that? Who *are* you?

I flung open the school door with a mighty push, hoping an afternoon breeze would provide some relief after the suffocation of the video lab. But it was one of those steaming fall days that made me feel like I might as well be back in Ahmedabad, and the dense, sticky air did nothing to improve my mood. At least I could jog a little on the way to pick up Pallavi from after-school. I needed to get out my energy.

Why oh why had Mr. Phillips assigned us partners? And why had he assigned me to Marina Glass? Did he think we had anything in common? Did he secretly want me to do a video on clothes? We were going to end up doing *Victim/ Victorious*, I knew it. Marina had barely said anything as I brainstormed, and I knew that she wasn't taking any of my ideas seriously at all. Everything I had done to get into Video seemed like a joke. Lying, sneaking—and making a video about clothes until Thanksgiving.

What did I have to say about clothing? My mom took us shopping twice a year in Queens, where the prices were cheaper, and my main fashion thoughts went something like, *This shirt basically looks like everyone else's, right?* The idea of me

Jessica Leader

helping to make a video where people decided what was hot and what was not would have made me laugh, except that it made me want to cry.

I ground to a halt as something lunged toward me—a taxi, careening into the intersection, its silver bumper giving off heat just inches from my knees. I started to back away, my hands held in the air, but the driver gestured in an irritated manner, *Go, go.* I bent my head and scurried across the street, mumbling, "Sorry," even though he couldn't hear me.

Yes, I thought, *exactly. Lunged at by a shiny silver Marina, and scuttling away.*

A warm breeze blew as I passed a fruit stand, giving me a breath of mangoes, just like in India. I missed India terribly. Things were so much easier there. No tests, no cliques—just my Nani's Best Movies of the Twentieth Century DVDs, going to the marketplace with my aunties, and playing in the courtyard with our cousins. Even though I hadn't lived in India since I was five, Nani—Ma's mother—really seemed to understand me. She was the one who had gotten me started making videos, when she'd asked me to tape Priyanka's fifth-grade graduation. And while the aunties had scolded me for cracking my knuckles—a habit I had started in sixth grade and couldn't seem to stop—only Nani had actually tried to help, offering me her gold and onyx ring if I could stop cracking by the end of the summer. I'd succeeded, but now I hoped that doing the video with Marina didn't zap away my powers of resistance. If I returned to Nani's home in Ahmedabad cracking my knuckles, I would spend the summer hanging my head in shame.

Pallavi's class burst out, a cluster of second graders dwarfed by their giant backpacks. I was skimming faces for my sister's when I heard voices chanting high above the crowd, "Pallavi is the princess! Pallavi is the princess!"

Pallavi, her own enormous backpack square against her shoulders, skipped in front of the singing girls. She turned to say good-bye and, to my amazement, they all curtsied! Pallavi gave a laugh that seemed to bubble up from deep inside her as her shiny black hair rippled down her back. She waved to her friends and ran over to me.

"Sa-cheese!" She gave me a jack-o'-lantern grin and her lunch box.

"Hi!" I said, bending down for a hug. "How was your day?"

She grabbed my belt loops and shook them. "I was the princess all day long!"

I laughed. "Wow!" I turned her around to leave the crowd. "How'd that happen?"

Pallavi took my free hand and gave a little skip. "I don't know! I just said, 'Who wants me to be the princess?' and everybody said, 'I do!' and so I was!"

"Oh!" Why couldn't my life be like that? If I said to Marina, or even Flora, "Who wants me to be in charge?" I doubted that they would respond by calling out, "I do!"

"Pul-vee!" sang a voice, and I turned to see Pallavi's friend Molly waving good-bye. "Don't forget to dress pretty tomorrow for your *boyfriend.*"

Pallavi burst into giggles. "He's not my boyfriend!"

Molly's dimples appeared. "I'm just *kidding.*" Over her head, Molly's mother made a face like, *Oh, kids,* and with all the maturity I could muster, I smiled. But inside, I thought, *Oh my word: Princess. Boyfriend.*

Was my little sister one of the popular girls?

"Matthew's not my boyfriend," Pallavi confided as we stepped out of the crowd. "He likes me, but I don't like him back."

"Oh." So she didn't have a boyfriend. She had something even better: a boy who liked her.

"Sachi?" Pallavi peered up at me as we waited for the light to change. "Do you have a boyfriend?"

"Pallavi!" I was shocked. "You're not supposed to ask questions like that."

"Boo." She kicked at the ground. "You never tell me any-thing."

I was about to say, *You're too young*, but then I remembered all the times my parents had told me the same thing, and how it had made me burn.

"Actually," I confided, "there is a boy I like."

"Really?" she shrieked. "Sachi has a boyfriend! Sachi has a boyfriend!" The light changed, and she charged across Seventy-third Street.

"Pallavi!" I struggled to keep up. "We're in public!"

"Who is he?" she asked, her eyes wide. "What's his name?"

"Alex." Alex Bradley. Just thinking his name gave me a thrill.

"Does he like you back?"

Why did she have to ask that? "We sit next to each other in English"—assigned seats, but still—"and sometimes, when he can't decide what to write about and I'm writing really fast, he says, 'Ms. Avery! You need to move my seat. Sachi's distracting me!'" My heart thumped as I thought about all the glorious times he had said that, the way his clear green eyes bulged out when he pretended to be seri-ous, and how the whole class laughed and I'd felt like a part of something.

"He says you're distracting him?" Pallavi wrinkled her little nose. "I don't get it."

The light changed. "Never mind." I hurried us across Second Avenue, where a bus waited several blocks ahead. And certainly never mind that he was going out with Elizabeth Ellis. Pallavi would probably think it was silly to like someone who was taken. She'd wrinkle her nose so fully, her face might never get unstuck.

We reached the bus stop, and as I fumbled in my bag for my MetroCard, I thought, if I were Alex, I'd pick Elizabeth over me too. Sure, she and I were both in honors classes, and both of us were nice—we had both won Nicest Girl in the poll, in fact—but there was something about her that said "Boyfriendable."

I'd thought about it in English, when Ms. Avery sometimes assigned me and Elizabeth to be partners. Yes, her jeans never sagged below her behind, the way mine did, and her hair fell into straight, even lines, while mine clumped. Yet I had this feeling that even if I managed to get my hands on a pair of the right jeans, or learned the secrets of the blow-dryer, I still wouldn't be Boyfriendable Sachi. The "right" kind of jeans would change, and clumpy hair would be the next cool thing.

How did people know these things? Elizabeth knew

them, and looking at Pallavi, whose hair was in mysterious new barrettes I had never seen before, I knew she knew too. It seemed to come naturally to them, the way solving an equation did for me, but there was no class in the world, not even an after-school activity, to help me catch up.

As the bus roared up to our stop, a thought popped into my mind: *Maybe I could learn about it in a class.* Maybe I could do it in Video. I ushered Pallavi into a seat and stood over her while the streets whizzed by. The video I'd liked so much from last year had had a funny beginning, but that part had been followed by interviews. Maybe Marina could do her *Victim/Victorious* scenes—whatever those were—and I could film interviews to stick in between.

I knew clothes didn't *make* you popular, and I wasn't interested in trying to start any trends. Still, I wouldn't mind knowing how Marina's friends all knew what to wear, or even how Flora and Lainey chose their strange styles. What made Lainey buy a bicycle-chain bracelet, and what made Flora choose that bracelet, out of the dozens in Lainey's collection, to copy? She liked it, of course, but it was probably more than that. She knew somehow that it was cool, and I wanted to know how she knew.

My video wouldn't have anything to do with people's nationalities, and that was a disappointment. But interviewing people about fashion would be better than standing around holding a camera while Marina directed them down a red carpet.

Yes. That was it. That was how I could care about our video. And if the bus didn't hit any traffic jams, I might beat my mother home in time to research it that very afternoon.

When we got back to the apartment, my research plans flew out the window. My mother was already bustling around the kitchen, and since Priyanka had a test the next day, I felt like I should offer to help with dinner.

I joined my mother in the kitchen as she pulled a pan from the lower cabinet, poured oil into it, and turned the flame on low. Grabbing onions from the hanging basket, I snuck a look at her. Some days she came home exhausted from the office, where the lawyers sometimes acted bossy just because she was a paralegal. She didn't seem particularly tired today, though—just her usual efficient self. Efficient enough, maybe, that she would want to bathe Pallavi while I snuck a little time on the computer.

My mom slid me a cutting board with a strong push. "So," she said, "you have some news?"

Her dark eyes were wide and ominous.

Oh no. Had Priyanka told on me? Why? I'd given her the

computer the night before without a single argument. Did she think I had told on her, and—

"The math test?" my mother asked.

"Ohh." I grabbed an onion from the basket above my head. "Ninety-five." Gripping the knife tightly, I chopped the onion in half. Calm yourself, Sachi. Spies are not lurking around the corner. Priyanka can be trusted. Probably.

"Not bad," said my mother, shaking some flour into a metal bowl. "But what happened? You said you knew the material perfectly."

"I got one wrong," I explained, piercing through the layers of onion, "and I didn't get the bonus problem right. Mr. Morrison said that you needed real algebra to figure it out."

"Hmm. Maybe you can ask him for practice problems."

"Maybe." I sighed quietly. I liked math, and I preferred hundreds to ninety-fives too, but I wished my mother could be happy with a ninety-five.

"Sachi." I heard a gentle *ting* as my mother set down the bowl and rested her hands on my shoulders. "I know we push you, but it is for your own good. I do not want colleges to say, 'She is the third-best Indian applicant from New York City—it's a shame we only need two.' I want them to say, 'She is the best!'"

I could have said this last part along with her.

"I know, Ma," I said. "I'll try to be more careful next time."

She kissed me, her cheek soft and dry against mine. "Good. When you finish the onions, would you like to roll out the chapatis while I run the bath?"

"Okay." I *do* like rolling dough. Priyanka and I always fight over it.

My mom glanced down at my cutting board and smiled. "Look at your beautiful onions! So even and fine, and you never shed a tear. You are going to be a great cook someday, and someone will be lucky to eat your meals."

I looked down at the slivers of onion. They had smelled sweet at first, but now they seemed rank. I knew my mom had meant to compliment me, but her vision of my future was depressing beyond belief. So I could chop onions without crying—would that help me work with Marina? Would it convince Alex to like me? Probably, while I was learning how to cut onions, Elizabeth Ellis's mother was helping her choose the most kissable lipstick.

My mother touched me lightly on the back as she squeezed out of the kitchen.

I threw the onions into the pan. They popped and sizzled. Now was my chance. I turned down the heat and snuck into the living room, where I seated myself in front of the computer.

First I typed in "popularity" and waited. Our Internet was so agonizingly slow! When the results finally appeared, I frowned. I did not want, as one site offered, to "measure the popularity of websites."

What about "clothing" and "popularity"? Strike two—it was all advertisements for clothing stores, each one claiming to have the hottest styles. I slumped back in the chair. Research for school was a lot easier. There was always a website on, say, Julius Caesar. I restrained myself from a knuckle crack and thought about how else to search.

"Sachi!"

I turned to see my mother standing in the living room doorway, her arms folded. "If I had known you were going to use the computer, I would have waited to cook the onions myself."

"What?"

"You didn't smell them burning?" She stalked back into the kitchen, and I followed to see her scraping crispy brown onions into the trash. "I don't know what you were doing on the computer, but it must have been fascinating."

"I'm sorry, Ma!" Here I'd meant to help, and I'd only messed things up. "It was research for school, and I didn't want to bother Priyanka—"

My mother snatched an onion from the basket overhead and began chopping it with quick, angry slices.

"I can do that," I said. "Really."

"Go do your homework, if that's what you need to do," she said. "I'll make dinner."

I didn't want to risk going back to the computer, so I picked up my things and trudged down the hall, my backpack feeling heavier with every step. As I passed our shrine, I offered up a silent prayer: *Raam, give me the courage to make this video. Because right now all I know how to do is make errors on my math test, look after my sister, and burn vegetables.*

MARINA'S LITTLE BLACK BOOK,
Entry #5

* Worst Homeroom Interruption: Rachel Winter
Can I have one day without this girl?
One day—that's all I ask.
* Best Homeroom Interruption: Sachi Parikh
Hey, what do you know?
She's useful after all!
* Most Unbelievably Beautiful:
Crystal Cabrera and Natasha Lambeau
If I have just one day where I look like them,
I'll die happy.
* Biggest Victim: Come On . . .
You Really Need to Ask?
Ha ha ha ha ha!

Wednesday morning, before the bell for first period, Elizabeth and I were just sitting in homeroom, talking about TV, when Rachel burst in. Her ginormous hairmop was barely held in place by two bright red chopsticks, and Addie was tagging at her heels.

"Reener!" Rachel cried. "Bird!" She was so loud that Ms. Avery looked up from her desk. *"Guess what?"*

I did not have a good feeling about this.

"What?" asked Elizabeth, leaning forward in her seat.

Rachel clip-clopped over and put a hand on her heart. "I just ran into Ms. Mancini, and she asked if I wanted to be the dance captain for *Grease!*" She clapped and squealed. "Isn't that the coolest? That means I'll get to run dance rehearsals when Ms. Mancini is working on other scenes! *And*"—she bent low to whisper—"that means more reasons I get to yell at Julian! Yay!"

She and Addie grabbed hands and jumped up and down together, like when my sister, Angelica, used to make me play ring-around-the-rosy.

I think Elizabeth said something like, "Rachel, that's awesome," but Rachel and Addie's giggling was damaging my ears. *Captain?* Julian was going to have an actual reason to listen to her now? So unfair!

Rachel's big scrawny hand clomped on my desk and pulled me out of my thoughts. "I have to get back to homeroom," she said, "but I'll see you girls later!" And she

and Addie were off, click-clacking toward the door in—
ew—matching zebra-striped flats.

I knew I should say something to Elizabeth so I didn't
look like I cared about Rachel's news. When I turned to her,
though, she was resting her chin in her palm and tracing her
other hand over some graffiti on the desk.

"Hey," I said, "what's going on?"

She kept tracing. "Oh, nothing."

"Lizza-Bird." I moved my desk closer to hers. "What?"

She shrugged. "I mean, not to be petty, but I've been
dancing longer than Rachel. I know I've got a speaking part
and everything, and I'm sure Ms. M. just wanted to make
things fair, but . . . whatever. I just thought she was going to
ask who wanted to do it, instead of picking randomly like
that."

I looked down at the words she was tracing—"Jasmine
luvs Danny"—and felt a boil of anger that Rachel could get
something Elizabeth deserved, probably just because Rachel
was loud. "Bird, hold on," I said. "You don't want the words
"Dance Captain" next to your name on the program, do
you? Seriously, what is that—like, you drive the ship?"

Elizabeth laughed a little, but she was still looking down
at the desk.

"Please," I said, "dance captain is no big woo. You've

got an actual part in the play. You get to sing on your own. People are going to remember that. If they remember the dance captain, it's only because she yelled at them for eight weeks straight."

Elizabeth tilted her head from one side to the other. "True," she said. "Actually, you're right. I would be too afraid of those eighth graders to boss them around, anyway. Some of them are scary."

I laughed. "Bird, you're so much cooler than any of them, any day of the week."

She smiled. "Thanks, Reener." Then she looked up with this kind of waiting expression on her face, and I turned and saw that girl Sachi on the other side of me. Oh, groan. I had already had enough interruptions for one day.

"Hi," she said, weaving her skinny fingers together. "Can I talk to you for a minute?"

I shrugged. "It's a free country." If she was going to make my day any worse, she was going to feel it.

"Um." She took a step closer. "I was thinking about it, and I decided we can make *Victim/Victorious* for our video after all."

"What? No way! That's great." Especially since I wanted more than ever to make fun of Rachel. Yes!

"I did want to say," Sachi added, "maybe I could—"

The bell rang, and everyone groaned and scraped back their chairs. "Hey, let's talk about it later," I told Sachi. I wanted to walk out with Elizabeth and think of more funny things to say about dance captains.

Even though Rachel had dominated Spanish with her super-cheese accent, I left class in the best mood. I had written almost half the script for the first scene of *Victim/Victorious*! There would be red-carpet shout-outs, Esmé winks, and everything else that was really on the show. Hot, hot, hot.

The best part, though, was that I had figured out how to make fun of Rachel's clothes. If I told everyone to dress up for the red carpet, there was no doubt that Rachel would bring in her most over-the-top, I'm-trying-to-be-cool out-fits. A few shots of those, a few scenes of her in barfarrific everyday outfits, and I wouldn't have to get someone to play a fashion victim—I'd have one right in front of me.

The plan was coming together, and if I got everyone orga-nized, I could start filming the very next day. I'd need that, because Video only went until Thanksgiving, and I had a lot of scenes to film. Maybe for once I could be one of those people who finished a project early. Ooh, and right down the hall stood the person who could help me make it happen.

"Hey, Sachi!" I called.

Ahead of me, Sachi froze, her books hugged to her chest.

I nodded in her direction as if to say, "Yeah, you." Was there some other Sachi I didn't know about? "Come here."

Sachi said something to her friend and walked slowly toward me.

"Hey, guess what?" I asked. I knew I sounded off-the-charts perky, but I didn't care; I just went ahead and told her the good news about the script. "Rachel and Elizabeth already told me that they could film tomorrow during lunch, so that's two people, and I'm going to ask the others later." Like Julian, and two extremely cool eighth graders. "Dance captain" would be old news before the day was through.

"And hey," I said, thinking aloud, "maybe today, when everyone goes to lunch, we can ask Ms. Avery if we can shoot in her room. You'd help me with that, right?" Teachers didn't like me, but any fool knew they looooved Sachi.

"Um," she said, "okay. And hey, I wanted to tell you this morning," she said, "I was thinking that maybe I could interview people about fashion and put them between your scenes."

I wrinkled my nose. "Why?" She would not bore up my video if I could help it.

"That video from last year had interviews. . . . I think people liked them."

"But that's not part of *Victim/Victorious*," I said, trying not to show how crazy she was making me. What was the problem with doing *V/V*? It was the woo of the century.

"People, the bell is about to ring!" Down the hall, Ms. Avery was sticking her head out of her room, her usual attempt to get us all into class. I didn't know why it mattered so much if we lost thirty seconds of English, but I didn't want any more trouble with Ms. Avery, so I told Sachi, "Look, just meet me in homeroom tomorrow during lunch. We can talk more then."

I seriously could not wait.

I glanced at the clock for the nine millionth time that lunch period, then slipped my cell out of my pocket and checked that, too. The school clocks were a minute and a half behind real time, but right now it didn't matter. Julian was officially more than fifteen minutes late.

"Marina?" Sitting on the desk next to me, Elizabeth said my name quietly, but even above Rachel's screeches, I could hear her. "Do you think we should just start?"

Her hair was starting to lose its wave. Next to her, Sachi's face had a pinched look, like she had chewed off the sides of her cheeks. "I've rehearsed it enough times with his lines," Elizabeth added. "I think I can do both parts."

I had so, so wanted for Julian to see the script I'd written, and to see that a *real* captain was more than someone who clutched your arm and laughed at you when you messed up. But if he wasn't going to show, I was just wasting time. "Yeah," I told Elizabeth, "I guess we should get started."

Elizabeth and Sachi hopped off the desks as I bellowed, "Okay, people! Let's do this thing!"

Everyone over in the Chatty Corner—my eighth-grade rock stars, Crystal and Natasha, and my plebes, played by Addie, Madison, and Chelsea—stood up. But Rachel put a hand on Crystal's arm. "Wait," she said, "finish the story."

Excuse me?

"Guys," I said. Was I going to have to go over there? "We only have fifteen minutes. Places!"

The plebes scrambled. But Rachel giggled, and I could have sworn I heard her say, "Well, if we have to get into *places*."

Crystal and Natasha headed toward the carpet, but I could tell they were snickering at Rachel's joke.

Whoa. Rachel had *not* just scored two new BFFs. I was the one who had crossed into eighth-grade lunchroom territory to recruit them. They were mine!

As Rachel walked to, yes, her place, I blocked her path, even if it meant coming face-to-face with her fake-pearl necklace. "What is your problem?" I said in a low voice. "You're totally throwing yourself at those girls. It's embarrassing."

Rachel pushed past me and said, "Oh, get over yourself, Marina." Then she glanced over toward Crystal and Natasha, like they were the ones she was really saying it for. Thank God they were fastening Natasha's bracelet and didn't seem to notice, but hello! This was my set!

I walked back over to my filming spot, flats clacking, to sit next to Sachi, who looked like she wanted to say something. "What?" I snapped, checking the camera battery.

"Should I fix the carpet?" she asked. "It's gotten kind of messed up."

"Oh . . ." She did have a good eye for that stuff, I noticed—she'd pinned my curtains to the window shade all artistically—so I needed to keep her in a good mood. "That's okay," I said. "I think people are about to stand on the carpet, anyway." That seemed to relax her a little, and phew. Her stressiness was stressing *me* out.

When everyone stood in their spots and had finished checking each other's makeup, I picked up the camera. Everybody was in focus. "*Victim/Victorious*," I announced, "scene one, take one." Hey, that sounded good. "And—action!"

Jessica Leader

Rachel and Chelsea walked by and waved and smiled at the camera. I kept Chelsea's little round face in the frame for about a second and then zoomed in on Rachel, starting at the bottom.

Crazy-tall spiked heels.

V-neck maroon dress with ginormous ballooning sleeves.

Strands of fake pearls, sparkly drop earrings, pounds of pearly eye shadow.

As she posed and blew kisses, I thought, *Rachel Winter, you are making this even easier than you know.*

Once I'd gotten enough victim shots, I panned back to Natasha and Crystal's walk. Right on cue, Elizabeth hobbled down the carpet to attack them for an interview.

"Oh, my!" she said. "It's Miss Crystal and Natasha!"

"Ojé, Mami!" cried Crystal.

Natasha struck a pose. *"Besos a tu madre!"*

Inside, I was cracking up. Sachi made a noise like she was swallowing a cough.

"You ladies get more fabulous every time I see you," Elizabeth was saying. "Who *ah* you wearing?" She gave a big wink to the camera, just like Esmé did ten times a night. I grinned into the monitor. I could feel Sachi crowding for a better look, and tilted the camera in her direction.

"I," said Natasha, "am wearing a very exclusive designer." She lowered her long, gorgeous eyelashes.

"And you, Miss Thing?" Elizabeth asked Crystal. That was Julian's line, and she sounded great.

"I just wanna say," Crystal began, "kisses to my man Big Kizzy, who—"

"Hey!" cried a voice. "What's going on here?"

I looked over my shoulder to see Julian Navarro, love of my life, vaulting over the desks and heading toward the back of the classroom. Now? He chose to show up *now?*

"Keep going!" I whispered to my actors, praying that I could edit my voice out of the movie. But Natasha and Crystal were waving to Julian, and Elizabeth was looking right at me with an expression like, *What should I do?* The take was ruined. They had totally lost focus.

"Cut," I called, and wanted to cry.

"Julian!" Rachel extended a knobby arm toward him over the desk she was leaning on. "You made it!"

He walked over and ignored her hand—yes! "Yeah, I made it. You guys started without me?"

What was I supposed to say? I didn't want to make him look bad, but I didn't want to make myself look bad either.

"Oh," I cried, upset like someone else had messed up, "I can't believe that happened!"

He ran his hands through his long black hair. "I tried to come upstairs earlier, but Mrs. Ramirez was like, 'Where's your note? Where's your note?'"

I thought I told you to skip lunch, I wanted to say, but I didn't want to fight with him in front of Rachel, who was licking her lips like she was about to get a treat. I needed to think of a new approach, and quickly.

"Hey, you know what I could really use?" I asked. "Someone to tell me how things look. Can you sit right here and be my assistant director?" I patted the desk between me and Sachi. Sachi had had her chance to watch the monitor. Now it was somebody else's turn.

A grin moved slowly across his face. "Assistant director? Ho ho ho." He walked around Sachi and sat next to me. "That, I can do."

"Great," I said, doing my best not to burst into a ridiculous smile. Take *that*, victim Rachel. "Let's just start from where Esmé says—"

"Wait a sec," Rachel interrupted, "I think it's weird."

Nobody ask, nobody ask—

"What?" asked Natasha.

Grr.

Rachel shrugged. "You know."

Oh, take your time, I thought. *We've got all day here.*

"That Scotty G wouldn't be at the Grammys," she continued. "I mean . . ."

"I can be in this scene," Julian said, looking from one of us to the other. "I mean, maybe I should."

I gave Rachel a murderous look she pretended not to see.

I turned to Julian and—boldness—put my hand on his shoulder. "I totally want you for the other scenes," I said in my sincerest voice. "But we've rehearsed this part, and—"

"It's okay." He hopped off the desk. "If you don't want me, I understand."

"Wow, Reener," said Rachel, "Way to take care of the talent."

"Okay, let's just do it," I said, ready to blow up. "Julian, take the microphone." We needed to get something real filmed today, if only so I could go home that night and find the moments where Rachel looked the worst, worst, worst.

The bell rang right after the shout-out, and everybody except Sachi abandoned me to get changed. It took us forever to put everything back, and by the time I got to the science lab, the bell had already rung, earning me my second late of the year.

"Tut tut," whispered Rachel as I slid into my seat. "Somebody needs to learn time management."

"*Some*body could have used a little help downstairs," I told her, wrestling my notebook out of my book bag.

Rachel just laughed like it was a joke.

Before I could think of a comeback, she passed me a note that had "White Pages, Volume 2" written on the cover. Volume 1 had been revenge plans for Señora Blanca ("Blanca" meant "white" in Spanish), and Volume 2 was slam notes about people in our classes. I didn't know why Rachel wanted to White-Page with me after being such a freak during my filming, but I was curious, so I opened it. Rachel had drawn a picture of Addie with huge cheeks and big black blobs next to her eyes. Underneath, it said, "Mascara boogers!"

I stole a look at Addie. Her eyes did not look that bad. Did Rachel think that Crystal and Natasha were now her BFFs, and Addie was her entertainment? I crumpled up her note.

Rachel didn't even notice. She was leaning over me to talk to Addie. "Addie," she whispered. "Go like this." She put a finger under each eye and wiped dramatically. "Boogers!"

Addie's hands flew to her face as if she'd been slapped, and smeared the black all over her cheeks. "Did I get it?" she asked.

"You look fine," I told her. She gave me a nervous smile. Poor Addie. Rachel didn't deserve her.

Yes. Rachel *didn't* deserve her. Revenge, part two.

"Adds," I whispered, leaning across the aisle, "come over after school tomorrow. I have the *best* idea."

Jessica Leader

SACHI'S VIDEO NIGHTMARE #6.0

INTERIOR. THE VIDEO LAB—DAY

Sachi and MARINA sit at their desks, facing
each other.

> SACHI
> So, I've been trying to tell you—I'd
> really like to film some interviews
> to go after *Victim/Victorious*.

> MARINA
> Sachi. There is no way I'm going to
> let you make my video look nerdy.
> And I would say I'm sorry about it,
> but really, I'm not.
>
> Here. Take this red carpet. We're
> going to shoot another one of my
> scenes.

As I stood at my locker, gathering books for Thursday
night's homework, my stomach started to feel hollow, and
it wasn't just because I hadn't eaten since eleven thirty.
Today was the day we were supposed to tell Mr. Phillips
our video topics.

English notebook, English folder, pencil case . . .

Marina's scene the day before had been funny. Even I had laughed at those gorgeous eighth graders acting like spoiled rock stars. But had I contributed one single thing, other than making sure no one tripped over the red carpet? No, I had not. I had had nothing to do with it, and it had had nothing to do with me. If I didn't get Marina to listen to me today, it would be ten more weeks of afternoons just like that one, and a video that embarrassed me more than a thousand pink tank tops.

On the other side of the hall, a door opened, and a laugh rose above the other sounds in a way that made me look over. Rachel Winter, her hair in poofy pigtails, was clutching Addie Ling and laughing so hard, she was almost choking. I had certainly heard *that* sound enough yesterday. Behind her, Marina seemed to be feeling the same way, and a grim look had settled on her usually pretty face.

I was about to turn back to my books when I noticed Marina talking to Lainey. Lainey drew back, as if Marina had said something mean to her, then dropped her gaze to the floor and continued down the hallway.

What had just happened? Did they even know each other? As Lainey passed by, I waved her over to my locker. "Hey," I said, "is everything okay?"

Jessica Leader

Lainey shrugged, making her bright green backpack twitch. "Just stupid people."

"What happened?"

"Oh, Marina just said, 'Nice shirt.' No big deal."

I examined her T-shirt, which was a pretty periwinkle and had a picture of tofu saying, "It's okay to eat me!" It seemed like a cute enough shirt.

"Why did she say that?" I asked.

"Who knows?" Lainey rolled her eyes. "Everyone at this school gives me such a hard time about how I dress. Just because I'm not Little Miss Preppy or Fashionista Wannabe . . ."

"I love how you dress!" I blurted out. In addition to the shirt, she was wearing a short jean skirt, pink high-tops, and black-and-white-striped socks. I didn't mean to sound dorky, but I didn't want Marina to get Lainey down. And the more I thought about the video I hoped to make (gulp), the more I realized that I didn't want to keep dressing in such boring clothes. A koala bear key chain wasn't the place to start, but how? "Where do you buy all that stuff, anyway?" I asked Lainey.

"There are lots of cool stores near my house," Lainey said, leaning her head on the locker next to mine. "Hey, do you want to come over this weekend? I *really* want to see the new Kyle Griffin movie." She fanned herself and added, "Hot!"

I giggled. "Maybe." I pulled my French book from my locker, my face warm from happiness. Lainey wanted to get together with me outside of school! I wasn't just Flora's friend to her. "Which day?" I asked, praying she would say Saturday. The past few Sundays, we'd helped my father clean out the back room of his jewelry store, then eaten dinner with our relatives in Queens. But before Lainey could answer, a voice said, "Hey, girls!"

I pulled my head out of my locker to see Flora bouncing up to us. "What's up?"

"I was just seeing if Sachi wanted to come to the movie this weekend," Lainey explained.

Oh. She wasn't inviting me alone. I set my backpack on the floor to zip it up.

"Downtown?" Flora seemed shocked.

"Yeah." Lainey looked down at me and back up to Flora. "What?"

"Nothing," said Flora. "I just don't think Sachi will be able to go."

"Why not?" I stood up. "Lainey, where do you live?"

"On Eighth Street," she said, looking hurt. "It's not dangerous or anything."

"No!" Flora's green eyes widened in protest. "I didn't mean *that*. Sachi just can't go that many places, that's all."

"Yes I can," I said, not believing she'd just told Lainey that. "I went to your uncle's play with you that time."

Flora shrugged as if to say that didn't really count.

"Let me ask my parents," I told Lainey.

"Okay, cool."

I put on my backpack, stung. It used to be that when I complained about my parents, Flora would complain about hers—"Those crazy Albanians," she'd say. They wouldn't even take her to PG-13 movies until last year. So why would she try to make me look bad in front of Lainey?

Suddenly I realized that the hall had almost cleared out. I glanced at the clock. Only one minute left until Video!

SACHI'S VIDEO NIGHTMARE 6.1

INTERIOR. THE VIDEO LAB—DAY

The bell RINGS.

Mr. Phillips shuts the door.

KNOCKING on the door.

CLOSE-UP: Sachi, her face pressed against the glass, pleading in silent desperation.

```
MR. PHILLIPS
Late, are you? You know what we do
to latecomers in this class.

MARINA (holds hands in air)
It's all Victim/Victorious, all the time!
```

"I have to go," I said quickly. "I'll ask my parents about the movie tonight. See you later!" Without even waiting for a good-bye, I slammed my locker door shut and bolted for the stairs.

When I got to the lab, every chair in the circle was filled except the one next to Marina. A quick glance told me that people were sitting next to their partners. I flew into the seat and said a startled "Oh!" as the person on the other side of me dropped a handout onto my desk. "Video Topic," it said at the top, and underneath was a list of things you needed to fill out about each scene: location, action, props. I peeled the top one off the stack and passed the pile to Marina. My heart, beating fast from the running, didn't show any signs of slowing. If I didn't get my ideas on this sheet, Mr. Phillips wouldn't know they existed, and I'd have no way to get Marina to include them.

The room was buzzing with partners talking excitedly— I overheard the words "rock star hamsters" and "the man with the hook"—but Marina wasn't even looking at me. Instead she was bent over her handout, writing in the space that said "Topic," "*Victim/Victorious*." Then, next to "Scene," she wrote, "One: Grammy Awards Red Carpet." She was about to write something on the next line when Mr. Phillips plunked his stool down in front of my desk. "Have you two decided what you're going to do yet?" he asked.

Marina passed her paper across my desk. "Yup."

My heart still pounding, I stuck my hand on top of the paper. "Um," I said, "not entirely."

Marina turned to me. "What?"

Mr. Phillips raised his eyebrows.

"I was hoping there could be a second part," I told him, trying to pretend that Marina wasn't there. "Like in that movie last year about where everyone sits in the cafeteria, they had interviews? I thought maybe I could do . . . interviews. That went after *Victim/Victorious* and sort of talked about how people decided what to wear." Now that I'd said it out loud, it seemed beyond silly. Priyanka would never speak to me after a video like that! I thought quickly and added, "It would be like a fashion investigation."

Mr. Phillips nodded encouragingly. "That sounds like a good idea."

I did not need to turn to see that Marina was not nodding encouragingly. "Wait, what?" she asked. "We haven't even talked about that."

The whole world seemed to be that white handout, lying diagonally across the cream-colored desk. "I did try," I said in a small voice. "I think maybe you just didn't hear me."

Marina clicked her pen. "Oookay."

"I really like your *Victim/Victorious* idea," I added, feeling like I needed to explain, "but I think interviews are a little more my . . . style." Not that she thought I had any style.

"Marina," Mr. Phillips said in an almost warning voice. "Does that sound okay to you?"

"If that's what Sachi wants," Marina replied.

What was the end of that sentence? *She's a huge nerd?* I hadn't meant to be sneaky, but I couldn't see any other way to make her listen.

Mr. Phillips stood up. "I can see that you are coming from different places, and sometimes video partners do divide and conquer, so it's fine that you're going in separate directions. Just make sure you help each other on your shoots, okay?"

I nodded. I wasn't sure what Marina did.

Mr. Phillips moved on to the next group.

"Great," said Marina, reaching over my desk to grab the paper. "Now we have to redo it."

"I don't think we do," I said. "You can have that part back, and I can plan my half on my own page."

My only answer was the sound of writing, scratchy like

the bug zappers in Nani's courtyard. Three guesses about who was the bug.

I should have been happy. I had gotten my idea into the video. I just wished I could have done it without making Marina think I was a sneak.

I stared at the blank space at the top of the page: "Topic." What *was* my topic?

Then I noticed the blanks next to the word "Scene." There were six.

Six?

I had been so busy nightmaring about *Topic*, I had barely thought about *Scene*. If I couldn't come up with anything, Marina would take over again with one of the many, many ideas that she was using to fill up her page. Our video was supposed to be only ten minutes long, fifteen at most, but hers looked like it could be a half-hour show all by itself.

I slid my hand into my backpack, unzipped my pencil pouch, and pulled out a pen. The pencil pouch, a birthday present from Pallavi, had pictures on it from the *Jabber Monkeys* cartoon, and now was not the time for Marina to sniff at one of my fashion choices. Still, that was just a mini-worry. The bigger worry was this: Whatever I did for my interviews needed to be really, really good.

MARINA'S LITTLE BLACK BOOK,
Entry #7

* Biggest Sneaky Kiss-Up Video Ruiner: Sachi Parikh
The teacher may love you, but that only gets you so far.
* Least Likely to Play Video Assistant: Addie Ling
But here she is.
* Most Embarrassingly Desperate: Marina Glass
Tell anyone and you're toast!

It wasn't until I'd looked through half the photos on my computer that I realized how late it was. Four thirty! I had wasted too much time updating the categories in my LBB. Addie would be here at my house in less than an hour, and I needed to get to work.

I opened my editing software and began adding the photos I had dragged into my "Video" folder. The pics of Crystal and Chelsea were nothing to slow down for, but all the ones of Rachel made me laugh.

The first was from the week before school started, with Rachel's hair bunched in pigtails that were *not* as cute as she hoped they'd be. I'd snapped the second just the other day— Rachel in crazy-tight pants and a nutty red belt that was big enough to be a Hula-hoop. The biggest prize, though, was Rachel in a loud-print halter top at sixth-grade graduation, looking down her nose like she was on the cover of *Vogue*. Those were the three best, and judging from the *Victim/ Victorious* clips I'd watched on YouTube, three was what I needed. It was funny—I couldn't even count how many episodes I'd seen, but I'd never thought about how they put it together before. Now I knew that they showed exactly three photos of past outfits worn by the main star of each episode. It wasn't the kind of info that would help me pull up my English grade, but it was kind of cool that I'd figured it out.

When I'd dragged my three photos into the slide show, I got to choose: Should the photos fade into each other, tile, or cartwheel? Cartwheel sounded like the most fun, but as I now knew from *V/V*, fading was the real way to do it. I clicked "fade" and sat back to watch the Victim-a-Thon.

Forty minutes later, Addie was sitting on my beanbag chair on the floor, iMovie was up on my computer screen, and everything was in place for me to hit "play." So why wasn't I showing her my video?

"It's just a rough cut," I told her, my hand hovering above the mouse. "I mean, I haven't even put in the sound." Addie didn't know it yet, but next weekend, when we went over to her place to get dressed before Caleb Rosenheck's Bar Mitzvah, she was going to hook me up with her brother's sound effects CDs. "I'm just saying, everything's not, like, completely perfect."

"'Rina." Addie elbowed my legs. "You know it's going to be good."

"No, I know, I'm just saying—" I know some parts are bad, and I'm working on them. "I haven't had time to—" Figure out when to start the music, or make sure I'd gotten the title color right. "You just need to remember that . . . Oh, forget it." If I couldn't show my video to a plebe, how could I show it to everybody in the Arts Assembly? "Here."

The video started black to be dramatic. Then, from either side of the screen, hot-pink letters faded in, reading "Victim/." Then, burning in slowly in bold, came the word "Victorious."

Addie clapped. "I love it!"

I bit my lip. So far, so good.

The screen flipped back to black. Red letters appeared, saying, "Starring your hot, HOT, HOTTTT hosts . . ."

Pictures of Elizabeth and Julian faded onto the screen.

Addie squeezed her hands into fists. "Eee!"

I grabbed my elbows so I didn't do my idiot grin. She was right, though. I had nailed the credits.

"Tonight's stars are . . ."

Three of Chelsea: fine, fine, and not too bad. One photo of Crystal, cut from the scene I'd shot the day before.

"Oh!" Addie pouted. "My face looks so fat!"

"What?" Her face was barely in the background. "It does not."

And then the Rachel photos.

After Rachel with the pigtails, Addie burst out laughing.

When she saw Rachel drowning in the Hula-hoop belt, Addie said, "Oh, wow."

And with Rachel in the halter top, Addie gasped.

The music faded and the screen froze. I waited.

And waited.

"I know it's not much," I said, "but I've really only been working on it since yesterday."

Addie shook her head quickly. "It's not that," she said.

What was her problem, then? "I know it's a little long," I said. Most *Victim/Victorious* credits were between sixteen and nineteen seconds—hello, squeegee. "But I wanted to include everyone."

"Oh." She was practically in a trance. "I didn't even notice."

"So?" I said. Was she going to make me ask? "What did you think?"

Finally Addie looked up at me. "Are you sure you should show that?"

I stared at her. "What?"

She pulled her knees up to her chest. "I just . . ." With her hair half-up and her little gold ball earrings, she looked more like a fifth grader than someone in seventh. "I mean, isn't she going to feel . . . you know . . ."

What, I thought, feel *bad*? The way Rachel makes me feel every time she brags about Julian? Or when she laughed after I told her my parents took away my phone as punishment for the poll? No, we couldn't possibly make Rachel feel *bad*.

"That was kind of the plan, Adds," I said, circling the mouse over the word *Victorious*. "That's what we talked about the other day. I mean, after what she did to you last weekend . . ."

When I'd told Addie what I was going to do with *Victim/Victorious*, she'd admitted that the weekend before, Rachel had invited her to her house in the Hamptons and then ditched her and invited Madison and Chelsea instead. "It's not right for her to dump you like that," I told her now. "You're her best friend."

"No, I know."

"Even Elizabeth thought you should say something," I reminded her, "and you know how much she hates in-your-face-ness."

Addie picked at her cuticles. "Yeah. I just—those pictures are so bad."

I was starting to feel weird sitting so high up, so I pushed back my chair and sat on the floor to face her. "She chose to wear those clothes," I told her. "It's not like we punk'd her, or put her head on someone else's body. We're just showing everyone what she chose to wear."

Addie didn't seem convinced, though. "I guess." She stuck the edge of her thumb in her mouth.

Oh, come on. Not just the sucking on fingers, but the poor, poor Rachel pity party.

Then I had a terrible thought: What if people agreed with Addie? What if they thought it was mean to show Rachel's ugly outfits? If I was the only one doing it, they'd all blame me. If it was me and Addie, though, we could say, "What? It was a joke," and people would believe us.

I hated to admit it, but I needed Addie. Plus, I needed her sound effects.

"Hey, you know what?" I said. "I have some cute photos of her." I hauled myself off the floor. "If you want, I can replace one of the photos with—hold on." I clicked around. "This one." It was a plain old shot of the four of us with Rachel in sweats, back before she chose to make her clothing a daily art project.

"Um," said Addie, "I guess that would be okay."

"Then I'll do it." It was a genius idea! Rachel couldn't complain as much if I showed a good picture of her. "I just think, Adds, you need to show her that she can't walk all over you."

Addie took her thumb out of her mouth. "I guess you're right."

I nudged her shoulder with my knee. "Of course I'm right. Nobody messes with Addie Ling."

Addie blushed. Even if, actually, people *did* mess with Addie Ling, she was on board. And that meant no one would mess with Marina Glass.

SACHI'S VIDEO NIGHTMARE #8.0

INTERIOR. JANE JACOBS MIDDLE SCHOOL
STAIRWELL—DAY

Sachi and Marina open the door to the
stairwell, carrying video equipment.

Eerie horror-movie MUSIC. Bats SCREECH.

The door SLAMS shut.

A THUMP—Marina drops the bag with the video
camera. She begins to strangle Sachi.

>   MARINA
>   Not only do I have to work on your
>   stupid video, but I can't even edit
>   my footage today? You're so dead.

Sachi gasps and sputters.

>   MARINA
>   (strangling)
>   Take that! And that!

Dead, Sachi slumps against Marina and slides
to the floor.

Marina picks up the video camera and tripod.

> MARINA
> Now I'm off to make the *real* video.

There were no bats in the stairwell, and Marina seemed only silent, not violent, as we descended to the basement, but I could feel her anger all the same. I had told Mr. Phillips that I didn't need Marina to come with me, but he had looked at me in surprise and said, "Partners film together." I knew that wasn't the answer Marina had wanted to hear, and with just the two of us in the dark, echoey stairs, I felt like I had to say something.

"I'm sorry Mr. Phillips wouldn't let you edit," I told Marina. "I'm glad you'll be helping me"—or perhaps not—"but if it had been up to me, I would have said you could stay upstairs."

"Whatever," she said. Then she muttered, "I don't know why you have to film during play rehearsal."

I hadn't expected *that*. "I don't *have* to," I said. "But that's where my friends are, and they said I could film them when they weren't onstage. I don't know when else I would do it."

Marina shrugged. "It's fine."

Okay. If it was fine . . .

I had to admit, there was another reason I wanted to

film in the auditorium: If Alex was on stage crew, maybe he would be around when I filmed. Carrying a video camera always made me feel slightly cool, and on top of that, I was wearing the black hoop earrings Lainey had bought me when I hadn't been able to come to the Kyle Griffin movie the weekend before.

Then again, I thought as I rounded a corner, *why should it matter which earrings I wore?* I didn't want to be one of those people who needed to be dressed a certain way to feel good. I ran my thumb over Nani's ring. It was all so complicated. Some days I truly wished I could go to school with my cousins in India. *They* got to wear uniforms.

And would I really learn anything from my video, anyway? I ran through my interview questions for what seemed like the twentieth time:

1. How do you choose what to wear?
2. Do you try to be unique, or to fit in? Why?
3. How do you think people decide some things are cool and some are not?
4. Do you know what's going to be popular? How?
5. Do you know what things are uncool? What makes them uncool?

I'd run the questions by Lainey in the hall before Video. "Yeah, these are fun," she'd said, handing them back to me.

"You're sure?" I looked at her closely. "They're not too . . ."

She pulled a book from her locker. "Too what?"

Dorky? Nerdy? Immature?

"I don't know." I tucked them back into my folder. "Thanks."

Flora had come loping down the hall just then, and I was glad Lainey was a fast reader. Even though I was going to interview Flora later, I didn't want to give her the chance to laugh at my questions.

Flora had said that rehearsal was mostly a nonstop festival of sitting around, but when Marina and I got to the auditorium, everybody was onstage singing this hoppy, boppy song. They sounded great! I wanted to leap up and join them. I glanced at Marina to see if she was feeling the same, but her arms were folded, and her jaw stuck out to the side. Oh, what was wrong now? Why did she always have to be in a bad mood?

When the song was over, a voice called, "Can I help you girls?"

As I looked for the person who had said it, there was a massive shuffling sound: everyone on stage, turning to look at me and Marina. Oh no! Was Alex up there? Had he seen me? There were so many people . . .

"Girls?"

Finally I realized where the voice was coming from: Ms. Mancini, the director, who was sitting in the audience. "Hi," I said, my voice sounding tiny in the cavernous auditorium. "We came to do some interviews?"

"And who said you could do that?" Ms. Mancini folded her arms.

I searched the stage for Flora and Lainey. "My friends?"

"Busted," said a voice, and everyone laughed.

"I don't have to do interviews," I said, my face feeling hot with shame. "I could just shoot B-roll, or not do anything . . ."

"B-row?" said Ms. Mancini, confused.

"Um, no. B-roll?" A few kids snickered. How horrifying, to correct a teacher! "You know, background shots?" I sounded like a huge nerd! Somewhere, Alex Bradley was probably laughing himself onto the floor. Beside me, Marina was scraping off her nail polish with the focus of a concert violinist.

"B-roll, right," said Ms. Mancini. "Well . . ." She turned behind her and looked at the clock. "We're going to do scene work soon, so why don't you set up your camera in the back, and when people are done, you can interview them."

"Thank you," I said, hugely relieved. "I really appreciate—"
She waved me away. "No problem."

I ducked my head and followed Marina, who was stalking

up the aisle toward the back of the auditorium. I hadn't even started filming, and already I was experiencing maximum humiliation.

After Marina and I finished setting up, she slumped into a seat in the back row and whipped out her phone to play a game. I watched her enviously for a moment, wishing my parents didn't consider cell phones to be "outrageous, expensive toys." Then I remembered—I had the best toy invented in my possession right at that moment: a video camera.

I turned around the tripod to face the kids onstage. It was cool to watch people without them knowing I was looking at them. I was like a giant eye, yet invisible. Too bad I still hadn't caught sight of Alex!

As I zoomed in on people in the crowd, I noticed a slight difference between seventh- and eighth-grade outfits. Except for Flora and Lainey, the seventh graders seemed to be more interested in looking crisp and neat, in dark jeans and colored tops, while the eighth graders looked sloppy but cool in sweatpants and T-shirts with the collars ripped out. Was being sloppy an older-kids thing? Would Marina and her friends start ripping their T-shirts when we graduated to eighth grade? Or was that just one class's style compared to another's?

Eventually Ms. Mancini said, "All right, folks—pajama party." People seemed to know what that meant, because everyone except the girls playing leads jumped off the stage and took a seat in the audience. Lainey stayed onstage —yay, Lainey!—and Flora joined a cluster of girls next to the stage with their scripts—understudies, I guessed. Some girls were coming toward me, and I realized it was Tessa and Phoebe from my math class. "Hi!" I whispered loudly, and waved. Once they got closer, I asked, "Are you here to be interviewed?"

They nodded enthusiastically, and my stomach did a little flip of joy. I was actually going to start filming! Then my stomach did a different kind of flip as I realized Marina would see me while I filmed. I glanced toward her seat, hoping she was still involved in her phone, but she was gone. I finally spotted her sitting over on the side with Addie Ling and some other girls.

"Should I sit?" Tessa pointed at the interview chair I'd set aside.

"Yes, please."

I shivered. This was really happening! The bargaining with Marina—the questions I'd prepared by flashlight— I was like an Olympic gymnast when it all came down to one big moment. I grabbed my clipboard of questions and hoped I could stick my landing.

"Ready?" I asked Tessa.

She nodded. Good.

Now, how should I start exactly?

Suddenly, I remembered a TV special I'd seen about filming the news. Just like the cameramen had said there, I said, "And five, four, three"—mouthed *two*, *one*, and pressed "record." My video had begun.

I tried to make Tessa comfortable by asking a few regular questions—her best subject in school, her favorite lunch. Then I started on the ones from my clipboard. "So," I said, "how do you decide what to wear?"

She frowned. "Do you mean, in the morning? I guess I look at the weather, and then—"

"Oh, not that," I put in. "I mean, when you're buying clothes. How do you decide what to buy?"

She hunched her shoulders. "I don't know. I guess I buy whatever's in the stores I like."

It didn't seem to mean much to her, but of course—stores! People went shopping together. Sometimes even after school, when I had to take care of Pallavi.

"How do you decide which stores to go to?" I asked.

"Just . . . wherever my friends and I go."

"But you don't buy everything." I hoped I could edit myself out of the interview, because I was talking way too much. "You must have a reason why you choose some things and not others."

She looked off to the side, and I started to worry that she wished she hadn't agreed to be interviewed. "I guess I just buy what looks good on me." She smiled. "And what my mom says I'm allowed to wear."

I smiled too, relieved and feeling brave enough to go on to the next question. "Do you try to be unique or to fit in? And why?"

"Um." Tessa chewed on her lip. "A little of both, I guess."

That made sense. Today she was just wearing a green shirt under a navy hoodie, but I'd seen her wear a gold-sequined belt like the other African-American girls in her clique. I was kind of hoping she'd say something about that, so I asked, "What makes you decide you're going to wear something trendy? Is it, like, a special day, or a certain thing you want to wear?"

"I don't know," she said. "I just do." Beside me, Phoebe had started texting. I knew I had better hurry it up.

"So, how do you think people decide some things are cool and some are not?" I asked.

"Um . . . maybe they read about it somewhere?"

"Okay!" I thanked her and pressed "stop." Phew! That was way harder than I'd thought it would be. But Tessa had always been kind of shy. Phoebe, who was next, wasn't shy at all. I hoped she would talk about the clothes she'd brought back from Japan. She had lots of things that no one else had.

I asked Phoebe a few of the regular questions. She had a really hilarious story about wearing an apron to school one day, and the interview was going so well that I started making up questions as I went along: "Have you ever noticed that people think some nationalities are cooler than others?"

Phoebe froze, like she did whenever a ball came toward her in P.E. "What do you mean?" she asked.

"Like, those Manga comic books are cool, but"—I had to laugh—"comic books about the Hindu gods are definitely *not* cool?"

She pulled her hands into the sleeves of her sweater. "I don't know. I'm not really into Manga."

"Oh gosh, I shouldn't have even . . . never mind." How could I have asked that? Hadn't Priyanka and I hated when people used to ask us to dance bhangra, since neither of us was a good dancer? "I just thought it was interesting that people are so interested in Manga," I told Phoebe, "and I wondered if you ever thought about it."

"Not really," she said. "But ever since I was, like, eight, people have been like, 'Ooh, bring me stickers when you go to Japan!' It's so weird that Japanese stuff is so popular.

I mean, I like it, but hello, I'm Japanese! I kind of want to say to people, 'Get your own stickers!' But it's also kind of cool."

I nodded. I kept having to remind myself that we weren't supposed to be having a conversation with the person we were interviewing.

Phoebe squinched up her face. "Is that it?" she asked.

"Oh—" I tried to come up with another question, but couldn't. "Yeah, that's it," I said. "Thanks." I switched off the camera.

Just then, the auditorium erupted in noise, and Flora and Lainey bounded up the aisle. "A break, finally!" said Flora, fixing her ponytail. "I thought we'd never be done with that scene."

I smiled. "So," I asked them, "who's going first?"

"Me!" called Lainey.

Flora stuck her tongue out, and they both laughed.

"Okay," I said. "Have a seat."

After I warmed up Lainey, I summoned my courage to ask her the question I'd been dying to ask her. "So. How do you choose what to wear?"

She shrugged. "I don't know. Some things just seem cool, so I wear them."

"Okay. Do you try to be unique or to fit in? And why?"

"I definitely try to be unique," she said. "Life is too boring when you dress like everybody else."

I wished I could be as confident as she was! "I was wondering," I said, making it up as I went along, "how did you decide to buy pink high-tops?"

Lainey was one of the only people in our grade who wore those sneakers, but they didn't look dorky, like Priyanka's old Reeboks. I really wanted to find out how people knew when originality was cool and when it was doomed.

She shrugged. "I don't know why I decided to buy them. People know that I wouldn't take pink seriously, so it's kind of like a joke."

A joke? Talking tofu was a joke, sure, but sneakers? "If another person wore them, would they be cool?"

She fiddled with her bracelets. "It depends on the person. If they were, like, babyish or trying to be cute, I wouldn't think they were cool, but maybe that other person would. I think it's all in how you look at things."

It was the perfect quote to end with. "Thanks."

"Whoa." Flora was staring at me with her mouth half-open, spiky hairs falling out of her ponytail. "What was that?"

"What do you mean?" My mouth suddenly felt dry.

"Those questions," asked Flora. "What is your video about, anyway?"

"Um . . . just . . . how people decide what to wear?"

"But . . . why?"

"Well . . . because that's what Marina's video is about. She's doing that show, *Victim/Victorious*, and I kind of had to do something like that. It's not what I would have chosen, but"—I threw a glance at Lainey, in the hopes that she might understand—"I sort of didn't have a choice."

Flora nodded slowly. "Okay." She took her seat on the interview chair. "I just . . . that's kind of weird for you, you know?"

I knew what she meant, but was I really too uncool even to wonder why people wore what they wore? Lately, talking to Flora felt like negotiating with a second Marina.

Once we started filming, though, she was great.

"I think people at our school get, like, these secret e-mails," said Flora, looking sly. "You have to subscribe on a website called Clones.com. Or Snobs.com. You have to have at least six Hollister purchases to get the password, and once you do, you get special e-mails telling you what's in and what's out."

I smothered a laugh. Still, how interesting! I had always thought that, like me, Flora couldn't afford to dress like the popular girls, or wasn't allowed. I never knew that she thought people who did it were dumb.

". . . and if they ever send me one of those e-mails,"

Flora was saying, "I won't be excited. I'll put it right where it belongs: the trash."

Talk about a great ending. "Cut!"

Flora grinned. "You're so official!"

"Thanks!" I checked the tripod, which had wobbled throughout her interview. Wait, I should have asked why she wanted to be different. Drat! Well, I could sit her back down again, right? Maybe *that* wasn't official, but—

"Sachi?" Lainey said.

I looked up. To my astonishment, three other girls I only sort of knew were leaning on the row of chairs, waiting to be interviewed!

"Hey," said one of them, chewing on a nail, "can we be in your movie?"

I flexed my fingers, dying for a good knuckle crack, while the next person took her seat. I was thrilled that people kept wanting to be interviewed, but no one was giving me any answers I could use. The video from last year hadn't had people stumbling over their words. Maybe they just had had an easier topic. But still, Marina's friends had had to memorize lines, and they'd done a great job! Marina and Sachi's video would come to be known as Partly Funny with Pretty Eighth-Grade Girls and Partly Boring with Lots and Lots of Talking.

"All right," called Ms. Mancini, "I need everyone up here for scene five."

"Oops." Lainey jumped up. "Showtime."

The crowd of girls scrambled down the aisle. "Meet us in the lobby later," Flora called.

I started packing up the video camera, looking around for Marina, when a familiarly scratchy voice behind me said, "Oh, so you're only interviewing girls? I see how it goes."

My stomach dropped into my feet. "Hi!" I said brightly as I turned to face Alex, who was leaning against the seats and grinning. "I didn't see you there."

"Yeah, the tech crew is pretty much invisible," he said, "but we have our ways."

"Um, that's cool," I said. I didn't really know what tech crew did, but I didn't think I was supposed to ask.

"So, can I?" he asked, gesturing at something.

"Can you . . ." Was he asking what I thought he was asking? ". . . be in my video?"

He nodded.

"Of course!" My cheeks felt hot again. Had I written any questions that boys would want to answer? "Have a seat."

As he walked over to the chair, I tried to ignore how incredibly cute he looked in his dark green sweatshirt, so

I could figure out what on earth to ask him. Did boys even think about their clothes? Did they talk about what was popular? I didn't know much about boys, but I was pretty sure they didn't.

"Is everything okay?" Alex asked.

I set down my clipboard on the chair next to the tripod. "Yup, everything's fine! So, I'm just going to . . ." Why could I say "And five, four, three, two" in front of girls I barely knew, but not to the boy I sat next to every single day? "I'll press 'record,' and the red light will go on, and then I'll point to you—"

Alex crossed his legs. "Yeah, I'm good. I've been video-taped before."

"Right." I tilted the camera downward, my fingers numb. What was I going to say?

"Um . . ." I pressed the "record" button. "So, I'm making this video about how people know what they like, and I wondered, how do you know?"

Alex chewed his lower lip. "I'm sorry, can you say that again?"

Not for a million dollars, it sounded so stupid. "People like all different things, right? Some guys dress like rappers"—yes, like anyone in our school dressed like a rapper!—"and some are more preppy, some are . . ." How *did* guys dress?

Our school wasn't like a Nickelodeon show, where one guy was sporty and one was skatey. "Anyway, I guess I'm just wondering, how do you decide"—what to wear? That was like asking him about being undressed!—"what look you want?" I finished lamely.

He hunched his shoulders. "I don't know," he said. "I just—if it's cold, I put on a sweater. If it's hot, I put on a T-shirt. I don't, like, think about it."

Maybe he didn't. But couldn't someone have given me an answer?

"Okay, cut," I said, letting out a breath. "Thank you, that was great."

His mouth was half-open, his green braces visible. "That's it?"

"Yup." Unable to stand the humiliation another moment, I switched off the video camera and clicked it off the tripod. "That's it."

"Okay, well, thanks."

"Thank *you*." I pretended to be incredibly involved with the tripod. My whole body seemed to be glowing with heat.

Somehow I made it back up to the video lab without dying of embarrassment. The Alex part of the day wasn't over, though. When I met Flora and Lainey in the lobby after the end of Video, something about their grins told me that the misery had only just begun.

"Sachi!" Flora bumped me with her hip. "Were you interviewing Alex Bradley?"

I checked my bag for my history folder, which I thought I'd forgotten. "Um. Yeah."

"Oh my lord," said Flora, "that boy has to butt into everything."

"No he doesn't." I found my folder and zipped my bag.

Flora shook her head as we pushed open the school doors. "You should see him in math. He has to raise his hand for every problem, even if he's wrong."

"Well, in English he writes really funny stories," I said, a sweat starting up on the back of my neck. Why did Flora think she was right about everything?

"Ooh!" said Flora, looking at me across Lainey. "Sachi, do you *like* him?"

"Yeah, do you?" Lainey asked.

"No!"

But I said it too quickly, and they both laughed.

Flora chanted, "Sachi has a boyfriend, Sachi has a boyfriend."

I hiked up my backpack. "You sound like Pallavi." And I had just sounded like Priyanka.

"Okay, never mind!" Flora rolled her eyes as we stopped at the light. "We were just joking. God, you're so cranky these days."

I was cranky? I could have said the same thing about her.

I *was* feeling grouchy on Tuesdays and Thursdays, though. There had been one beautiful moment today, shooting B-roll. My real footage and everything that went with it was like D-roll. D for disaster.

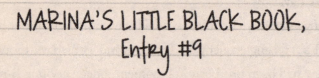

MARINA'S LITTLE BLACK BOOK,
Entry #9

* Most Annoying Hairdresser: Bianca Glass
Come on! Just say yes!
* Most Surprising Hottie: Jake Ling
Look out, Julian!
* Worst Choosers of a Time to get Rhinestones:
Addie Ling, Marina Glass
How could they have known? And what can Marina do?

I slipped my new dress into the garment bag my mom had lent me. It had taken me three shopping trips to find the perfect Bar Mitzvah outfit, but I had done it: black satin with subtle, silver-thread stitching and a delicate scoop neck. Tonight was going to be hot, hot, hot. I zipped.

My duffel and purse were packed, and my hair was feeling dry enough, so I went back into the bathroom to use the straightening iron. Usually I just blew my hair dry, but tonight I wanted to put my hair up in a half bun with the rest of my hair hanging stick-straight around it, and that took work. I sat on the toilet, plugged in the straightener, and waited for it to heat up while I listened to Angelica's SpongeBob movie drift down the hall.

Twenty minutes later, SpongeBob had figured out the mystery of the missing Krabby Patties, but I was still sitting on the toilet, with the smell of toasted hair stinking up the bathroom. The stick-straight thing was not working at *all*. One side looked squashed and limp, while the other side kept curling out. I looked at my watch. Crud! Addie and I were supposed to start the anti-Rachel sound effects in twenty minutes, and every extra minute here meant chunks out of the half hour before Elizabeth and Rachel came over. Even if I took a cab to Addie's, I would need to get going soon.

"Mom!" I yelled. Sometimes she was good at hair emergencies.

"Whaa-aat?" came the reply from her end of the house.

"Can you help me with my hair?"

"Come in here!"

I groaned. "Can't you come in *here*?"

She didn't even answer. "Poop," I muttered, turning off the not-very-straightening iron. She and my dad were going to some benefit that night, but that didn't start until seven. I had to leave *soon*.

I slumped into their room with my lame, hot straightener in hand. "It's not working," I said, sitting on the bed.

"Be careful of my dress!" My mother ran over to me in her slip and stockings, a blush brush in one hand.

I looked at the plum-colored dress on the other side of the bed. "I'm nowhere near it," I said. "Can you help me with my hair?"

She lifted parts of it with her free hand. "What's wrong with it?" she asked.

"It's totally flat on the left," I said. Someone who spent as much time on her hair as she did should know *that*! "And see how it's all wavy on the right?"

"It looks fine," she said, sitting down at her makeup table. Why did people always open their mouths when they put on eye makeup? "It has a natural wave."

"I don't want a natural wave!" I said. "That's why I have the straightener." Duh! "Can I just plug it in and you can help me? You did it for Annabelle's wedding." My cousin's wedding had probably been the one and only perfect hair day of my life.

"Your dad is using the bathroom right now." My mother sifted through her makeup drawer.

"So just come to mine! Please? I have to go in, like, five minutes."

"Can't you wear your hair a different way?"

"No! I want to wear it in a half bun, and the rest has to be straight." That was the whole concept!

My mother slammed the makeup drawer shut and stood up. "Marina, I don't know why you have to make such a production of everything. It wouldn't kill you to—"

Blah blah blah. At least she was going to help me. I followed her into my bathroom and didn't even complain when she almost burned my neck. Twice.

"Bye, guys," I said to Angelica and her babysitter, grabbing my coat from the hall closet. They were eating hamburgers in front of the TV.

My mom came padding down the hall in her bathrobe. "Here," she said. "Cab fare."

"You're not going to come down with me?" I asked. Last year had been the first time I'd been allowed to take a cab alone. My mom had made a huge deal of always putting me in a cab with a "nice" driver, whatever that meant.

She waved me away. "You'll be fine for one night."

"Oh." I pulled my coat out of the closet. "Okay." I didn't know why I cared—not like I wanted to spend more time with Bianca Glass. I just—I don't know. Thought she might want to see me off to the big Bar Mitzvah or something. Even if I was just starting off at Addie's.

"Marina," said Angelica, "will you bring home your party favors?"

"No, I'll leave them there," I joked.

Angelica blinked, surprised.

"Marina." My mom gave me a sharp look. "There is no need to be obnoxious."

"I was *kidding*."

"She's too young to understand sarcasm." My mother broke a dead leaf off the flower arrangement on the coffee table.

"Forget it," I muttered. "Angelica, I'll give you anything I don't want."

Angelica pulled the blanket over her knees. "Thanks."

They were so annoying! I couldn't deal with kissing anybody good-bye, so I pulled on my coat and left.

When I got to Addie's house, the first person I saw after Addie was her older brother, Jake, wandering around the living room.

"Hi," I said, keeping my voice down as I took off my coat. "What's *he* doing here?"

"He's leaving soon," Addie whispered. "He can't find his wallet."

Jessica Leader

"I'm leaving, I'm leaving," Jake said, looking under a stack of magazines.

Addie whipped around. "We just want some privacy, Jake. Is that so much to ask?"

"It is," he said. "I really want to watch you guys do your makeup."

I laughed as Addie handed me a hanger.

He found his wallet and walked toward the coat closet, leaning past me to grab a jacket. Yowza! I hadn't seen him since before the summer, and he'd grown a lot. His hair had grown too, and now flopped over his eyes in a way that was just complete hotness. If this was what happened to guys once they hit tenth grade, I'd definitely stay in school.

"Just don't let me catch you in my room again," he told Addie, pulling on a black fleece (preppy but manly.) "I don't know how long I spent picking your gum out of the carpet."

"That was in fifth grade!" Addie cried. "God, you always—you just—"

She looked at me helplessly.

"Gross," I said. "As if we'd even want to go into your room." I ran a hand over my supersmooth hair.

He laughed and slid his wallet into his back pocket. "You're bad, Marina," he said, and picked up his backpack. "I'll see you guys later."

"I'll see you *tomorrow*," Addie yelled out the door. "We're staying at Elizabeth's tonight!"

"Whatever!" he called as the elevator door opened.

Addie closed the door, and for some reason, we burst out laughing.

"Can we get it?" I asked. "His computer?"

She nodded. "My stepmom's at the grocery store, so we need to do it now."

Fifteen minutes later, we were laughing hysterically in Jake's room. "You have to burn me this CD!" I said. "I mean, how much better would your life be if you got to listen to this every day!"

I pressed "play" so we could hear "Barf #3": *Bleh, bleh, bu-le-huuuuuuh . . . plunk plunk plunk.*

Addie burst into giggles. "Or no, wait, let's try this one." She pressed "Fart #4": *Ffffff . . . doink!*

I held my sides to stop them from hurting. I knew it was not exactly the most sophisticated thing in the world to laugh at the sounds of barfing and farting, but it was just not what you expected when you sat down at your computer. And especially not Jake's computer.

"Okay, so let's see where we should *put* these sounds," I said, loading my DVD into the disc drive. This week in class

I'd finally gotten to work on my video a little. I had to admit, Mr. Phillips's editing program was much better than the one I had at home. You could slow things down a lot more and take out bad light or weird sounds. This meant that the red carpet scene wasn't a total waste—no thanks to my biggest victim.

"This is cool," I said when the video popped onto the screen. "I think I know a few places where we can play these sounds. What if . . ." I dragged the sound files into the frame-by-frame lineup. "What if we do this?"

I pressed "play" on the red carpet scene and watched everybody strolling by. Then, when I did the close-up on Rachel's heels (so nice and slow! Excellent job, Marina!), we heard the sound of "Barf 1," the quick little *Bleh*. When the camera showed her balloon sleeves, there went "Barf 2," a slightly longer *Bleh-heh-hehhh*. And for the fake pearls and eye shadow, "Barf 3:" the *Bleh* with the plunking. I grinned.

"You're not really going to do that, right?" Addie tugged on her gold chain, which did not go at all with her pink sweatshirt.

"Um, yeah, that was the idea," I said. "Come on, it's hilarious."

"You're going to do it for other people too, though, right?" she said. "So it's not just about Rachel?"

"I have to make it about Rachel," I told her. "Otherwise, we have no victim."

Addie picked at one of the stickers on Jake's computer—MR. ZOGG'S SKATE WAX, it said in big yellow letters. "She hasn't been that bad since the whole Hamptons thing," she said softly. "Maybe that was just a misunderstanding."

"What?" I asked. "You did not misunderstand her uninviting you. Come on, you said you were going to do this. You can't back out now." No one ever wanted me to have any fun.

"Hey," called a voice. "Can somebody come help me with these groceries?" Addie's stepmom, with perfect timing as usual.

Addie turned to me, panicked. "I'm not allowed to be in here," she said. "Um—"

"Here," I said, and clicked the video shut.

It wouldn't close.

"Hello?" said Addie's stepmom again. I heard a sound like grocery bags being thumped into the apartment. "Anybody home?"

"You go help her," I said, giving Addie a nudge. "I'll get this out."

"She'll hear you." Addie stood up. "The kitchen's right out there."

Did I have to figure everything out myself? Times like this, the "Biggest Plebe" thing really made sense. "Go meet your stepmom in the hall," I told Addie, "and give her a big hug and go slow walking into the kitchen. I'll put Jake's computer in your room and we can get the disc out later. Okay?"

Addie breathed a sigh of relief. "Thank you, Reener," she said, and fled.

I unplugged the power cords, clutched the laptop with my baby inside—which I'd better be able to get out of the disc drive, hello—and dashed through the kitchen, past the dining room, and into Addie's bedroom. As the door swung shut behind me, I heard Addie's mom say, "Thanks, honey. Just be careful of the rip in that one."

Phew.

When the doorbell rang ten minutes later, I still hadn't gotten the DVD unstuck. "Marina!" Addie wailed. "When are you going to get it out?"

"It's fine," I said, really tired of the mini heart attacks. "The real thing is at school." I wasn't actually supposed to have made my own copy, but what Mr. Phillips didn't know wouldn't hurt him.

"Addie!" called Addie's mom. "Your friends are here."

Someone giggled, and Addie and I whirled around to see Rachel and Elizabeth in the doorway dumping their bags on the floor. Elizabeth's hair framed her face in beautiful blond waves, and Rachel had the stick-straightest blow-out I had ever seen.

No. Way.

"Hey!" said Addie, coming forward to hug them. "You guys look great!"

I closed Jake's laptop behind me with a click. How could Rachel and I have had the same hair idea? Did that make me victim-licious? Mine was the only one in the half bun, but her hair was ruining my effect.

"*Your* hair looks great, Bird," I told Elizabeth.

She smiled. "Oh, you too!"

I came toward Elizabeth, ignoring Rachel. Rachel's face was so thin, the flat-ironed hair made her look like my cousin's poodle after his bath.

As I went to hug Elizabeth, she stepped back. "Hey," she said in a joking voice, "don't mess the do."

"No, no, of course." I leaned in and gave her an air kiss.

"You really think it looks okay?" Rachel was asking Addie.

Elizabeth groaned. "As I told you five million times in the cab, yes, it looks fine."

I burst out laughing. Elizabeth, giving Rachel a hard time? What was that about?

"I don't know," said Rachel, taking a seat on Addie's bed, looking shrunken and wounded. "The whole thing was so traumatic."

"Oh, Ray-Belle." Addie sat next to her. "What happened?"

Prediction: This story was going to involve everybody worshipping Rachel. I leaned against the desk and mentally signed up for a barf bag.

"My mom took me to her hairdresser," Rachel said (spoiled show-off), "and the stuff they put on it smelled like that acid we used in science, and they got some on the back of my neck, and it totally burned me!" She turned around so Addie could see her neck. "Look!"

"Ow!" said Addie, leaning in. "Do you guys want to see?" she asked me and Elizabeth.

Elizabeth gave me a little smile like, *Oh, gosh.* "Um, I already saw," I told Rachel.

Addie dropped the chunk of Rachel's hair. "Poor you!"

"The stylist didn't think so," Rachel said, finger-combing her hair into place. "She kept laughing at me."

"What?" I asked. Someone else thought Rachel was ridiculous? I should get her number.

"She was like, 'Oh, it doesn't hurt, it doesn't hurt, sh-sh-sh.'" Rachel mimicked the woman, waving her hands like she was putting out a little fire. I laughed, wishing I'd been there.

"Then," Rachel said, "at the end, when I said, 'I think there's something wrong with my neck,' and she saw the burn marks, she was like, 'Oh, that happens to some of our clients, but you'll be fine.' She completely blew me off—twice!"

"That is pretty evil," I admitted. "I would have told my mom not to tip her."

"Oh, I did better than that." Rachel grinned. "They gave me tissues, because I was crying, so I crumpled them up really small and left them in the mints jar at the front desk."

"You did not!" I cried.

"I totally did!" Rachel's smile stretched all the way across her narrow face. "Somebody is going to have a delicious surprise when they reach for a post-haircut breath freshener."

I cracked up.

"I can't believe you did that!" Addie cried.

"That is gross," Elizabeth declared, folding her arms.

Rachel and I were still dying. "I know," she said, "but that woman deserved it."

"I think it's awesome," I told her. Elizabeth being grossed out didn't bother me, but I was sick of Addie's Careful Routine. "I should add that to White Pages, Volume One."

Rachel cackled. "Hey, Adds," she asked, "did you get a new computer?"

Addie flinched. "What?"

Rachel pointed at Jake's laptop.

"It's Jake's." Addie started picking at her fingers, and I thought, *Stop it! Touching those cuticles is a dead giveaway!* "He was just, um, showing me something."

"Oh." Rachel tossed her hair. "I was going to say, those stickers are so not you."

"Oh, yeah. Ha!" Addie gave a lame laugh, then looked nervously at me.

I didn't want everyone staring at the laptop, so I walked over to the other side of Addie's bed and lay down. Elizabeth sat next to me with her back against the headboard.

"I'm *tired*," said Rachel, flopping onto her stomach to face me. "I almost don't even want to go tonight."

"No way," I said. "Really?" I was feeling kind of cozy too, but I still wanted to go to the Bar Mitzvah party.

"Yeah." Rachel picked at a loose thread on Addie's comforter. "I don't know, it's kind of nice when it's just us, away from everybody."

"It'll be fun when we get there," Elizabeth said.

"No, I know," Rachel answered.

As the room fell silent, I watched Rachel's silver fingernails picking at the thread, surprised at what she'd said. She was the one who'd wanted to hang out with the eighth graders during my shoot, or that time I showed up at rehearsal. Was she getting tired of trying to be Most Popular? Hey, I didn't mind keeping the title. I was psyched for the party. But Rachel really did look droopy, and not just because of her hair. For a minute I felt bad for her.

"Come on," I said, nudging her elbow, "you know you want to go."

She shrugged. "Yeah, I know."

How could she forget our joke from last year? "No, I mean, you *really* want to go."

A smile cracked across her face. "Hmm, I don't know . . ." Good, she did get it. "I'm not sure I do."

"No, you *know* you do." I propped myself up on my elbows. "You've been, like, fantasizing and dreaming about this moment your entire life, and now it's actually going to happen, and you cannot wait."

"You really can't," Addie put in, and Rachel, Elizabeth, and I burst out laughing, because it was so unexpected for Addie to say something like that and get it right. My eyes landed on Mr. Jolly, Addie's ancient stuffed frog, sitting on the shelf above her bed. He may have been babyish, but tonight, I wanted to give him a hug.

"You know what we need?" Rachel bounced up onto her elbows. "We need something to set us apart. To show everyone that we're, like, the four besties."

"Like what?" Elizabeth scratched her neck lightly. "We don't want to make people feel left out."

Leave it to Elizabeth.

"Nothing major." Rachel tapped a silver nail against her teeth, thinking. "Just something—"

Addie jumped up. "I know! I have the perfect thing. It's in my parents' room."

"Ooh, I want to see!" I said. "I'll come with."

"My stepmom got these stick-on rhinestones in a magazine," Addie whispered in the hallway. "You put them under your eye, right here." She tapped her cheekbone.

"Woo!" We slipped into her mom's room. Two scores for Addie in one night—who knew? We agreed that Addie would wear the rhinestones into her bedroom, since they were hers, and then the rest of us would all put them on together.

"Check it out," Addie said, and did a very *Victim/Victorious*–like strut down the hall, her hips snaking back and forth, her arm snapping over her head.

"Go, Addison!" I giggled. "Hey, girls," I called as we came into the bedroom. "Check it out."

Rachel and Elizabeth had moved to the computer, and they whipped around when we walked in. Their mouths fell open. And I realized what they had been looking at while Addie and I had been dancing.

Behind them, the screen flashed a slide show of pictures I knew way too well: Rachel victim pictures. From where I stood, the soundtrack was tinny, but I could have sung along with every single photo.

"Omigod," Addie said. "How did you—you guys weren't supposed to—"

"We just wanted to hear Jake's iTunes." Elizabeth's voice was a whisper.

Rachel twisted back to the computer and hunched in her chair. Elizabeth turned away from me and put her arm around Rachel.

I ground my feet into the carpet. I wanted to run from the room, but I was sewn to the floor. *Don't be mad,* I wanted to say. *It was an accident. You weren't being fun when I did this. It's not my fault.*

Before I could say anything, Rachel turned back to face us, her eye makeup smeared. "What were you guys doing?" she asked. "Is *that* Marina's video? Addie, are you helping her?"

"No!" Addie cried. Then she looked at me. "I mean, Marina wanted to use Jake's sound effects, but I told her I didn't want to work on the video anymore. I was going to tell you!" she said to Rachel, sounding like she was going to cry. "I just didn't want to tell you tonight."

"What?" I asked. I couldn't believe she'd flat-out deny it. "That is so not true," I told Rachel. "She was totally helping me."

"Why would you even do something like this?" Rachel asked. Elizabeth stared at me with round eyes, like she was wondering the same thing. "What did I ever do to you?"

Air blew in from the window. Somewhere in the apartment, a door closed. "I don't know," I said. I had meant to get Rachel upset, but I had never thought about what she would look like when it happened.

"Are you mad at me?" she asked.

"No," I muttered. "No."

"So you just did it for fun?" Rachel's voice croaked.

Yes? Or more than that? "I don't know."

"Then why?" Rachel looked at Addie. "Just tell me."

Addie gulped. "She said you were getting too bossy."

Rachel's mouth dropped open. "*Marina*, you thought *I* was bossy?"

"I don't know." Outside the window, pigeons squawked. "Kind of."

"So you made a video about the way I dress?" She stared at me like I was insane. "What is that? You're the one who always says you hate followers. I try to be a little different and you make me look like a freak?" Her voice cracked.

"Rachel, we love the way you dress." Elizabeth knelt next to her. "You're just who you are, and that's amazing. No one else does what you do."

Just because Rachel was crying, she was amazing? Whatever!

"I think you dress great too." Addie ran to her side. "I'm so sorry! I don't know what I was thinking. I just—we got carried away. But we'll totally erase it, and—"

"Oh, please," I burst in. "Addie, you're not even going to tell her why you're mad at her? You have, like, no backbone at all."

"Marina, stop!" Elizabeth cried. "Don't make things worse."

"Whatever." I folded my arms. "But I don't know why you're being so nice to her, Addie. You should hear what Rachel says about you."

"What do you mean?" Addie looked from Rachel to me.

"Ask Rachel." I nodded in her direction. "Maybe you want to know what poll categories she thought you'd win before the two of you get all lovey-dovey."

"Marina." Elizabeth's mouth was a tight line. "Do *not* go there."

"Go where?" Addie's gaze bounced back and forth between us. "What categories?"

Rachel smeared her face with the side of her hand and sat

up straighter. "You agreed with me, Marina." She thrust her head forward, just like she did when she lied to teachers. "I was joking, but you wanted to put those categories in there."

"What are you guys *talking* about?" Addie's voice sounded strained—great. Was she going to cry even before we told her about Biggest Plebe?

"Look," Elizabeth broke in, "they didn't do it, so don't even worry about it. And Marina," she said, her gaze landing on me, "you can't show people that video."

"That's my property," I said. "I worked hard on it."

"You can still keep the good parts, right? Can't you have a different victim?"

"It's my video." I did not like her telling me what to do. "I can do whatever I want with it."

"But why do you have to do—that?" Elizabeth asked.

"Because I do," I said. If she didn't get it, I couldn't explain it to her.

"Why does everybody have to be like this? Just—trying to get each other all the time." With her wavy blond hair, standing by the chair in her washed-out jeans and off-white sweater, Elizabeth looked like she was visiting from someplace where it was still summer. "Sometimes I can't fall asleep because I'm thinking about all the things I said that day and how you're going to get mad at me."

Really? *Elizabeth?*

"Me too," Addie squeaked. "Some nights I can't even fall asleep."

Okay, now that was just the peak of raging ridiculousness. They were just trying to make me feel bad. "Look," I said to Addie, "don't pretend you didn't want to get Rachel back. And Elizabeth, I'm sorry if you got upset, but that's how the world works, and if you're too nicey-nice to—"

"What do you want from us?" Elizabeth burst out.

It took me a second to realize she was talking to me. "What?"

"You just have something bad to say about everyone." Her voice wobbled. "If you hate us all so much, why are you friends with us?"

Wonderful. Let's all cry because of Marina.

"Seriously." Rachel wiped her nose with the back of her hand.

"Yeah," Addie said.

They all stared at me: Rachel with her smeary cheeks, Elizabeth with her pinched face, and Addie with her eyes all droopy and sad. I started to feel hot and starved for air, like the time in second grade when I threw up in music class.

"Oh, like you all don't bad-mouth each other all the time." I shook my head. "I've heard you all, every single one of you."

No one said anything.

I rolled my eyes. "Great. Thanks a lot. Thanks, all of you." I grabbed up my bags and stalked out of the apartment without even looking at them.

The sky had turned that creepy blue you get on fall afternoons, but it was barely five o'clock, and the party wouldn't start for another two hours. A few cars slid down Park without any traffic to stop them. The only other person on the street was a man walking his dog.

Heading back to Angelica and her hamburger would be beyond depressing. I couldn't lower myself by going to Madison's or Chelsea's, and Rachel would probably text them that I was evil, anyway. I tried to rest against the ledge carved into the building, but it wasn't wide enough to hold me, and the stone dug into my thighs.

Where was the party, anyway? I fished the invitation out of my bag. DISH RESTAURANT, it read in raised maroon calligraphy, FORTY-TWO EAST FORTIETH STREET. Like I even knew what the city looked like down there. *The restaurant had better be cool,* I thought, running my fingers over the creamy paper. How pathetic would it be if the first Bar Mitzvah of the year was held someplace totally un-hot?

Hey! I knew someone who lived near there: Sachi. When we did a number puzzle with palindromes in math—Mrs. Ramirez's idea of a fun treat—someone had mentioned that

Sachi lived on Thirty-Third and Third. I had never heard of anyone living in that neighborhood, which was why I remembered it.

I whipped out my phone, thinking, *Yes.* I could just chill at a squeegee house. No fashionista wannabes, pathetic puppy dogs, or goody-goody traitors. I would enter the party refreshed and cool. Nobody would expect me to, which would make it even cooler.

I called information for Sachi's number and walked up the street as the phone rang. A grown-up answered. He had an accent, and at first I thought I had the wrong number, but then I remembered, duh, Sachi's Indian.

"Hi," I said, "can I speak to Sachi please?"

"Who is this?" The voice did not sound happy.

"This is Marina." I checked my hair in a car window. "From school," I added when he didn't say anything. "From her video class."

There was a pause. "Sachi is not in a video class."

"The elective," I said. "With Mr. Phillips. At Jacobs Middle School?" Had I gotten the wrong number?

"Just a moment, please," the man said, and then I heard him call, "Sachi!"

I shook my head. The life of the non-cell-phoned.

"Sachi," said the voice, "what is the meaning of this?"

SACHI'S VIDEO ~~NIGHTMARE~~ LIFEMARE #10.0

INTERIOR. SACHI'S KITCHEN—EVENING

Close-up: Sachi's mother's hands. They throw
a ball of dough against the counter and shape
it into a flat, perfect circle.

Sachi and Priyanka, cooking. Pallavi, underfoot.

The phone RINGS.

Sachi, her mother, and Priyanka continue
their work.

    SACHI'S FATHER (*off-camera*)
    Sachi!

Sachi looks questioningly at her mother, who
takes the spoon from her.

    SACHI'S MOTHER
    He sounds upset. Go.

Sachi wipes her hands on a dish towel and exits.

My father was standing with the phone pressed against
his chest, forks and knives lying in piles on the table.

"Sachi," he demanded, "what is the meaning of this?"

His tone chilled me. "What—what do you mean?"

He stared at me with hardened eyes. "There is a girl on the phone."

"Yes?" Was I supposed to know what he was talking about? "Who?"

"Marina. She says you are in a video class with her." He spat the words.

Like the time on the street with the taxi, I froze. "I—I, uh—"

His glare didn't soften. "This is what you have to say?"

Before I could come up with anything, my father put the phone to his ear. "I'm sorry, Sachi is not able to talk to you right now. Can she call you back?"

I could hear talking on the other end. "I see," said my father, and then again, "I see."

He rested the phone back against his chest.

"Your friend Marina is in an emergency," he said, "and I am going to tell her she can come here."

"Marina Glass?" Why would Marina—

"Afterward," my father continued, "your mother and I will have a long talk with you about this *video* class."

He returned to the phone.

SACHI'S VIDEO NIGHTMARE #10.1

Black screen.

The sound of a heart, BEATING fast.

A rush of WIND.

CUT TO: a video camera, surrounded by flames.

CUT TO: Sachi, motionless.

A BEEP. SACHI'S FATHER hangs up the phone.

"Neeta," my father called. "Make a few extra rotis. Sachi has a guest coming for dinner."

My mother came around the corner and into the living room, slapping a chapati back and forth between her hands. "A guest? Now? Who?"

"Sachi's friend Marina," said my father, folding his arms, "from her video class."

The chapati flopped over my mother's fingers. "What do you mean, video? I thought we settled that ages ago."

"Sachi?" asked my father. "I think you have something to tell us."

I knew they expected nothing less than a full explanation,

so I went ahead and told them: "I forged the signature on the permission slip."

"You *what*?" My mother's voice sliced the air like a knife. "You forged the signature? You deliberately disobeyed? That is completely unacceptable! What child of mine—"

Darkness seemed to fill the space around my head.

"Pallavi, no!" Priyanka's voice rang into the living room.

"Aagh!" Pallavi shrieked.

Priyanka thumped in from the kitchen. "I told Pallavi not to pour the oil, and she did, and now it's all over the floor."

My mother made a sound of exasperation. "Pallavi, come out here. Tanish, will you—"

"Of course." My father walked briskly toward the kitchen. Pallavi came running out, her shirt covered with oil and her face streaked with tears. "I didn't mean to," she sobbed.

My mother motioned her over and began wiping Pallavi's hands with her apron. "Sachi," she said, "go finish helping with dinner. We will talk about this"—her mouth tightened—"video business later."

When the doorbell rang, I raced to answer it. I needed to intercept Marina before my mother could glare in her direction.

I threw open the door to an unusual sight: Marina, with fancy hair, weighted down by two large bags and a purse. Was she running away? Had there been a fire? Where was her family? And how long was she planning on staying?

"Hi," I said.

"Hi."

I waited. Didn't she want to explain what was going on?

"Is everything all right?" I asked finally.

She shrugged. "I'm fine."

I stepped back so she could fit through the doorway. "Do you want me to hang that up?" One of the bags was the kind my mother used to store her fancy saris, and Priyanka and I didn't have room in our closet for something that big.

"No, thanks," said Marina. "I'm going to put it on soon. I just need to stay here until, like, 6:45. Then I have this thing to go to."

"Oh." A *thing*? What kind of a thing? I couldn't believe she wasn't going to tell me what was going on. "Is everything all right?" I asked again. She didn't look like she had been crying. "My father said you had an emergency."

A flush colored her creamy complexion. "It's not really an emergency," she said. "I just needed someplace to go."

So you came here? I wanted to say. *You don't even like me.*

"Sachi." My mother came out of the kitchen, her apron

covered with flour. "You are not going to introduce me to your friend?"

"Friend." If the situation had not been so awful, I might have laughed. "Ma-ji," I said, using the formal expression, "this is Marina Glass."

Marina held out her hand. "Nice to meet you."

I cringed, knowing that just moments before, my mother had been blotting chapatis with a paper towel. I hoped she hadn't gotten any grease on Marina. And that Marina knew the salwaar kameez under my mother's apron was Indian clothing, and not what Pallavi had once called "funny pajamas."

My mother's eyes were traveling over Marina's bags. "Sachi," she said, "you'll need to change the sheets on Priyanka's bed."

Marina started to say something, but my mother cut her off. "Priyanka," she called, her face turned toward the kitchen. "You'll be sleeping in Pallavi's room tonight."

"What?" Priyanka came through the swinging door drying a bowl and wearing an irritable expression. "You're letting her have a sleepover just like that? Oh," she said when she saw who it was. "Hi."

"Hi." Marina shifted her bag like it was straining her arms. "I'm Marina."

Priyanka's eyes stayed fixed on Marina as she rubbed every last drop of water from the bowl. "I know."

"Oh." Marina was obviously embarrassed, and I wanted to sink into the floor. I didn't think you were supposed to admit that you knew people if they didn't know you.

"You don't need to worry about sheets," Marina told my mother. "I just need—I mean, I was hoping—" I had never seen her stumble over her words before. "Sachi's dad said that I could stay here before I go to this—thing."

My mother raised her eyebrows. "A 'thing'?" I guessed I wasn't the only person not satisfied by Marina's explanation.

"Um, a Bar Mitzvah?" Marina said it like a question. "One of those parties for when Jewish kids—"

"I know what a Bar Mitzvah is." My mother did not sound amused.

"Oh, okay, well." Marina seemed to disappear into her bags.

"Sachi, give your friend a place to put her belongings," my mother said. "Dinner will be ready in five minutes."

As Marina followed me down the hall, I wondered why she hadn't just told me about the Bar Mitzvah. Was she afraid I'd be jealous? All right, I was, but that didn't mean she needed to act secretive.

I opened the door to my room and was hit with a flash

of panic. My *Jabber Monkeys* pencil case sat right on top of my backpack, and Ganesha, Priyanka's stuffed elephant, was fully visible on the bottom bunk! I was sure Marina didn't have anything like that in her bedroom, and I didn't want her to tell people about my babyish things.

"Here, you can hang your dress in the closet," I told Marina. While her back was turned, I stuck my pencil case in my backpack. I was debating what to do with Ganesha when my mother called, "Dinner is ready!"

"Come on," I told Marina, "let's go."

As Priyanka and I carried bowls to the table—my mother wouldn't let Marina help—Priyanka hissed in my ear, "You'd better not tell Ma and Papa that I knew about Video."

"I won't," I said impatiently, then tried to smile as I set the rice in front of Papa. Gosh! Did Priyanka really think I was going to begin the conversation by saying, *Have a nice meal, everyone—by the way, Priyanka let me bribe her?* I wished our seats weren't across from each other so I didn't have to look at her.

As we began passing around the food, my mother explained each item to Marina, just as she always did to our non-Indian guests. "Okay," Marina kept saying, and then another "okay" when my mother asked if she wanted some of that food on her plate. I guessed it wasn't any different from when Flora came over, but Marina seemed like the kind of person who would whisper about it to other kids in school. And that went double when we started eating with our hands—though my mother had provided Marina with a fork and spoon.

Pallavi acted silly the entire time, purposely eating with her left hand until my mother gave her a look. As soon as she switched to her right, she asked Marina, "Are you sleeping over?"

"No. I'm—going out," Marina said with a wary glance to my parents, as if she knew they thought it was strange.

"Where?" Pallavi asked.

Marina took a forkful of rice. "A Bar Mitzvah?" She said it like a question.

"What's a par mistfah?" Pallavi asked.

Marina giggled. "Bar Mitzvah."

Pallavi tucked her legs underneath her so she was tall enough to lean on the table. "Far blitsfah?"

Marina shook her head and smiled. *"Bar. Mits. Vuh."*

Pallavi grinned, showing her newly missing front tooth. "Par. Bits—"

"No!" Marina laughed. "Bar—"

"Pallavi, that's enough," my mother said. "You can practice saying it later."

Pallavi's face clouded. She smeared her hand around on the plate.

Across the table, Marina hunched over her food, her eyes cast down. I couldn't believe her! Couldn't she see it wasn't a joking evening? Even Flora knew enough to act formal in my house. It was just Marina, with her giant bag and fancy hairdo, who didn't seem to realize what was going on.

When Marina and I got to my room, I was dismayed to see that it was only six fifteen. What would we do for a whole thirty minutes? But Marina was all business, bending to open her duffel bag, rifling through her clothes, and pulling out several pouches, including one that must have contained pounds of makeup, it was so large. I pressed my ring deep into my finger. I was going to have to watch her put on makeup, and she had no idea what she had done to me. Life to her was just one huge makeup bag and Par Blitsfah.

Finally she stood up, clutching her pouches to her chest. "Should I get ready in your bathroom?" she asked.

"Um . . ." I shared the bathroom with my sisters, and I did not want Pallavi bursting in on her. On the other hand, I wasn't sure where else to put her. It wasn't like Priyanka and I had a table devoted to putting on makeup.

"Here." I unplugged the lamp from my desk and put it on top of my bureau, next to my mirror. "Is that okay?" I hoped Marina would be done before Priyanka came in and accused me of moving the entire room around.

"Um." Marina looked it over. The reflecting light made the wall shockingly bright, but I didn't know where else I could set up. "Sure." She headed over to the corner of the room and took out what seemed like dozens of tubes, pots, and brushes, all glossy black with thin white writing. Even my mother didn't have that much makeup, and hers was all unmatched and ancient.

I thumped down onto Priyanka's bed. Ganesha fell onto his side, and I shoved him into the corner with my elbow. How could Marina have spent so much money on a thing like makeup? It was all I could do not to give my knuckles a good crack.

Marina noticed me looking. "Do you want some?" she asked, holding out a brush.

My face grew hot. "No, thank you." Of course she thought I wanted what she had. I turned on Priyanka's bedside lamp, grabbed the nearest book from her shelf, and pretended to read. The sounds of my family washing dishes drifted down the hall, and I hunched deeper into the pillow, trying to push aside my thoughts about what would happen once Marina left.

After a moment I realized that what I had taken was Priyanka's French book, and that I must have looked pretty stupid reading *Le Petit Prince* for fun. But who cared—who on earth cared what Marina Glass thought after what she had done? Ignoring the click of makeup pots, the zipping of bags, and the crinkling of the dress, I read every word on the page, whether I understood it or not.

"Well, I guess I should get going," said Marina finally.

When I glanced up, a gasp escaped my lips. I didn't want to think so, but—Marina looked beautiful. Her dress clung in a way that gave her just a little bit of shape. Her shoulders emerged from the top of the dress as smooth and round as scoops of ice cream, and the hanging wisps of hair that had looked so strange before now framed her face like it was a portrait in a museum. I suddenly became aware of my baggy gray sweatpants and Priyanka's YMCA T-shirt and pulled my top closer around me, desperate to look like anything other than a child in her pajamas.

She tugged her dress downward. "What?" she asked. "Do I look okay?"

That did it. I crushed my palm against my knuckles in a great loud crunch. How dare she ask me that? She knew she looked beautiful. She had swept into my house and blown my secret and gotten my little sister in trouble, and now she

Jessica Leader

was trying to get me to tell her how artful her makeup was, how perfect her hair? I wouldn't. I refused.

"You look fine," I told her stiffly.

Her gaze fell to the carpet, and she returned to her duffel bag. "I should get going."

I turned back to Priyanka's bed and stood Ganesha up on four feet. So what if Marina knew Priyanka slept with a stuffed animal? There were things in this world that she knew nothing about.

The walk down the hallway felt like a march to my doom. Part of me was shouting, *Go! Go! Go!* The other part pleaded, *Don't leave me alone with my parents.*

As it turned out, the leaving was delayed, because my mother bustled in from the kitchen and insisted that she ride in Marina's taxi to the party.

"She's allowed to take taxis on her own," I protested. I couldn't imagine what Marina's friends would think if they saw her getting out of a cab with my mother.

"It's no trouble," said my mother, heading for the closet. "I'll take her."

I was trying to come up with a response when Marina said, "It's fine. I don't mind."

Thank goodness for that. Although she would probably

tell all her makeup-wearing friends how my parents treated me like a baby.

My mother opened the door, then paused with her hand on the knob. I knew what she was expecting me to say. "Thank you for coming to dinner," I told Marina. I wanted to add, *And for ruining my life*.

"Thanks for having me," Marina replied.

"Tanish," called my mother, "I'll be back in a moment. Sachi, will you finish up in the kitchen?"

I nodded.

The door swung shut, sending Marina and my mother out into the night. Except for the rumble of the dishwasher, the apartment was silent.

Behind me my father said, "Go clean up. We will talk when your mother returns."

"Yes, Papa," I said, and headed into the kitchen to face the grime.

MARINA'S LITTLE BLACK BOOK,
Entry #11

* Thrower of Biggest Pity Party That Gets Everyone
on Her Side, Even Though She Totally Doesn't
Deserve It: Rachel Winter
People are BLIND if they can't see that she brought
this on herself!

* Biggest Dupe: Elizabeth Ellis
Dupe: n. One who is easily tricked or fooled by
others. (I looked it up.)

* Coolest New Friends: Olivia and Annalise
Who's applying to private school next year? Marina
Glass. See ya, suckers!

Monday morning, I hopped off the Madison Avenue
bus, pumped by the music from the Bar Mitzvah CD.
The party had been raging. I'd made these awesome
new friends from Marlowe, this hot, hot, hot private

school, and was already planning to apply next year.

Rachel, Elizabeth, and Addie were drooling with jealousy, and they deserved to be, after acting like monster drama queens all night. Pulling plebes into the corners and whispering, then turning around to give me mean looks? Please. Like I actually cared what Madison and Chelsea thought of me. I would so ditch them for Marlowe kids, ASAP.

I crossed Seventy-Ninth and headed for the bus shelter, and oh, great: There was Elizabeth. With the collar of her pale blue trench turned up to her chin and her earbuds tucked in tight, she looked like her mind was far, far away. I had hoped I could avoid her by being late, but I guessed she was running late too.

Well, no big woo. We'd have to make up sometime, and I could be the bigger person today.

I scooched past a woman in ugly sneakers to stand next to Elizabeth. At first she didn't look up. I waited. Then I started getting impatient and leaned into her. "Hey," I said. "Anybody home?"

Her eyes widened, like I was the last person she thought she'd see. "Oh," she said. "I didn't see you."

Did she really think I'd fall for that? Oh, Elizabeth.

"How *are* you?" I pulled out my own earbuds and pasted

on a fake smile. I thought it would be good to let her know I was still a little mad.

She didn't answer because the bus pulled up just then, and she got busy winding up her earphones. The door opened, and I saw that it was the nice driver with the beard—a good sign. He smiled as he saw us.

"Hi, ladies," he said. "How are you doing?"

"Fine," Elizabeth said politely, "and you?"

Good, she wasn't in a bad mood.

I looked up from dunking my MetroCard, and whoa! The bus was packed. Usually we liked to stand in the back half but today we had to push and crush just to find standing places away from the door.

The bus lurched away from the curb, and we grabbed handles. "Holy bejeezies!" I cried, expecting she would laugh. Elizabeth stared straight ahead as if I hadn't said anything. Ugh! Was she going to do this to me the whole ride? Okay, so we'd had a fight, but come on. Whose best friend was she?

"Hey, did you do the social studies?" I asked. Usually I hated when people talked about homework on the bus, but I knew it would put her in a good mood.

She pushed her hair out of her eyes. "Yeah."

"What did you put for why Caesar crossed the Rubicon? I don't think it was even in the book."

She shook her head. "I don't remember."

"Oh." The bus zoomed across Park Avenue—my favorite part of the ride, because it was like two blocks in one, and you felt like you were actually moving.

"Can you believe Caleb's low-rent party favors?" I asked. "I liked the CD, but the rest of the stuff was so junky."

Elizabeth's eyes flicked toward me. "I thought they were okay."

"Temporary tattoos? Hello, third-grade swag."

She shrugged.

As my mother had said to Angelica this morning, "No more grouching." Could I not say one thing that Elizabeth would talk about? I'd had enough.

"Okay," I said, "what's wrong? Did you not get enough sleep or something? You know we had that talk about going to bed on time."

"Marina." She bit her lip. "You were really mean to us on Saturday."

"What? Omigod, like you didn't say anything mean?"

"You called me a goody-goody," Elizabeth said. "That's not, like . . . I don't know. Nice," she whispered, looking at her feet.

Oh. Right. I *had* said that.

Okay, then.

"Look, Bird," I said, "I was freaked out. I was surprised.

I didn't mean everything I said. You know that, right? So, I'm sorry. Okay?"

She looked down, then shrugged. "I just . . . you know."

"What?"

"I mean, thank you for apologizing, but . . ." She fiddled with the belt of her trench coat. "That video thing. That was, like, a big deal."

First of all, it was not a "thing." And second: "My video has nothing to do with you."

"Yes, it does."

I squinted. "Why?"

"Because of Rachel."

I rolled my eyes. Yes, let's not forget about Rachel, who was so devastated on Saturday night that she didn't stop her little hand-jive dance at the DJ station until he gave in and handed her a prize.

"I'm sure she's thrilled to invite everyone to her pity party," I said, "but there's more than one side to this story. Did anyone even say, 'Wow, you went on Addie's computer and looked around in her files?' That's, like, breaking and entering. I think you can get sued for that."

"Well . . ." Elizabeth opened the top button on her trench coat. "I still saw it, and I don't know . . . you and Rachel are friends."

The bus pulled over by the flower shop on Lex.

"Friends don't sneak onto friends' computers and watch videos that aren't finished," I told her. "I was going to tone it down before I showed it to people. It's like—when Ms. Avery says you have to get all your ideas out in the first draft. That's what you guys saw. A first draft." Oh, so cool that I could compare Video to English, which Elizabeth loooved. Hot.

"I know, but still." Elizabeth tugged on her collar. "She saw it. She was really upset, and you didn't exactly apologize. And, I mean, if you would do something like that about her, and plan to show it to the whole school, what are you saying about the rest of us?"

"But I would never say anything about you." Why was that not obvious? "It's just Rachel. Do you not see how she's become a total attention hog and fashion 911 case?" Not to mention the way she'd tried to steal Crystal, Natasha, and Julian. And also—"She's not just rude to me. You were the one telling Addie to say something after Rachel uninvited her to the Hamptons. This is just a way to settle the score. For me *and* for Addie."

"'Settle the score'?" Elizabeth grimaced. "I'm sorry, Marina, but that's kind of scary."

"It's just an expression," I said.

She didn't say anything.

"Wow." My mouth tasted like Sour Patch Kids. "I can't believe you're on her side."

Elizabeth inched back to avoid a seeing-eye dog. "I'm not exactly on her side," she said, her eyes following the dog, "But—look, Marina . . . I was going to say, when I first saw you . . . I think I just need a break."

The dog's tail thunked against my leg. "A break from what?"

"From . . . you."

I stared at her. "What? I make a video about Rachel, and *you* can't be friends with me? What is that? She is so evil! I swear, Bird, you have to listen—"

"Marina, I'm sorry, I've thought a lot about it, and I need more time to think. I'm not saying I'm on anybody's side, and I'm not saying I like her and not you or anything like that. I just need a break."

"Omigod." I shook my head. "You watch way too many *Friends* reruns. Just—"

The door opened with a burst and a hiss, and I realized, *Crud, we're already at school.* As I pushed our way to the front door, people gave us nasty looks, but it was too crowded to fight our way to the back.

Once we were on the pavement, Elizabeth said, "I don't

think you should show that video. Not just because of Rachel. I heard about something like this at another school, and the person got into major trouble."

My head swirled with comebacks about the video, about how she was in it herself, about how wrong she was. "Look, you don't—wait. Just let me explain—"

Elizabeth looked down at the sidewalk. "I'll see you later, Marina."

The bus roared away, blasting my leg with hot exhaust. I watched Elizabeth walk down the block, dodging the squeegees and their wheelie backpacks, her straight blond hair angling toward the ground.

"Thanks for the advice, counselor!" I called.

That was it. I was transferring to Marlowe faster than Rachel could choose another victim outfit. Maybe they even accepted you in the middle of the year.

SACHI'S VIDEO NIGHTMARE #12.0

INTERIOR. MR. PHILLIPS'S CLASSROOM—DAY

Mr. Phillips sits at his desk, reading. Sachi
trudges in and hands him a sealed letter. He
opens it and reads.

     MR. PHILLIPS
     You lied to your parents to get
     into this class? You're pretty
     desperate, aren't you?

Sachi's face contorts in pain.

     MR. PHILLIPS
     And I've heard something else
     about you today too. What was it?
     Oh yeah: Your older sister is a
     nerd, and your parents are way
     overprotective. Letting you into
     this class was obviously a big
     mistake. Let me write myself a note
     so I don't let you in next year.

"Second Avenue! Everybody off for Seeecond Avenue!"
It was the crosstown bus driver who thinks he's a radio

announcer. Sometimes it cheered me up, but today it didn't. I mumbled "Excuse me" to the orange-haired woman next to me and slogged off the bus, my parents' letter burning a hole in my book bag.

My father had handed it to me as I'd left for school. One more humiliation to end the worst weekend of my life. I walked down the block, my head swirling with all the events that had followed Marina's departure.

With every grain of rice I swept, every counter stain I scrubbed, nightmares flooded my head. Would my parents accept my apology? Could I possibly, possibly stay in Video? I hadn't exactly gotten the answers I wanted from my interviews, and after tonight the thought of being Marina's partner worked me into a speechless rage. I liked Mr. Phillips, though, and I liked what we were learning. I knew it was crazy, but I didn't want to give it up.

Finally, when the dishwasher ground to a stop, the surfaces gleamed with Soft Scrub, and the floor shone spotless, I knew I couldn't put it off any longer. I ran a rag around the rim of the sink and dried my hands on a dishcloth. The time had come.

My parents sat at either end of the dinner table, sipping tea. They did not suggest I pour myself a cup.

"Sachi." My father's cheeks hung heavily from his face.

"We are very disappointed in you. Your mother gave up her legal practice back home so we could move here! You know how late I work at the store so we can stay in Manhattan. Do you think we do all this so you can make videos and lie to us?"

A lump rose in my throat. I hated thinking about everything they had given up for me. I missed our relatives all the time. To know that they felt it too made me wish I had never even heard of video class.

"I'm sorry," I whispered. "I didn't do it to be disrespectful. I just—wanted to—" Blinking back the tears made it hard for me to speak.

"Will you explain to us, first, please," said my mother, "why it was necessary to do exactly what we asked you not to do?"

My gaze fell to the table. I had never noticed the waves in our wood, like the topographical maps we had studied in science. I wished I could ride them and sail away.

"Sachi?"

I couldn't answer my mother's question. Despite what I had thought in the kitchen, now my reason seemed unimportant. "I was wrong," I managed to croak out. "I'm sorry."

"I am glad you are sorry," said my father. "I only hope it is not too late to make up what you have missed. On Monday you will go to the test preparation class and ask if you can be included."

I nodded. "All right."

"You will have to work very hard to catch up," my father intoned. "No computer, no phone calls. You must catch up on studying for the test."

"Okay." I loved my twenty minutes of phone time each night, but I deserved to be punished. "I do know test prep is important. I've been studying on my own."

"That is not as good as being in the class," my father warned. "You need to do what the teachers tell you. They are the ones who can help you learn the tricks."

"I know." I looked up at last, glad to assure him of something. "But I won't be too far behind. I'm using Priyanka's books."

This time my father's face showed surprise. "What?"

"I—" Oh no. I hadn't meant to . . . oh no.

My mother gasped. "Priyanka lent you her books?"

I couldn't lie again. "Yes."

My mother held her hand to her chest. "So she knew you were lying to us?"

"I . . ." Oh no. No! "Yes."

My father smacked his palm on the table and turned away from us, pressing his hand against his moustache.

"Both of you." My mother seemed to be in a daze. "Both of you were lying."

I bent my head.

"Priyanka!" My father's voice roared through the house.

"Yes?"

"Come in here, please."

I pressed so hard into Nani's ring, my index finger burned. Priyanka entered, wary.

"Priyanka," my father instructed, "sit down."

She obeyed.

"Sachi tells us she has not been in the Test Prep class. That she has been doing this video class instead and you knew."

Priyanka bowed her head. "Yes."

"So." My father's wide fingers stroked the glossy wooden table. "You knew and you didn't tell us. You deliberately deceived us."

"It was Sachi's idea." Priyanka's chair creaked. "I was helping her. Doesn't that count for something?"

"But you lied to us!" my mother cried. "You both lied!"

"What was I supposed to do," said Priyanka shrilly, "tell on her? When Sachi doesn't get her way, she makes my life miserable."

"What?" I broke in. *"I make *your* life miserable?"*

"Don't try to make *me* look bad!" Priyanka shot back. "See if I help you with Test Prep ever again. I hope you *don't* get into Stuyvesant, so I don't have to see your face for the next three years."

"Stop it!" my father thundered. "We did not raise you to talk to each other like that."

"She started it," said Priyanka. "She's the one who—"

"Girls, that's enough," my mother said. "It's late, and I don't want your sister to hear you arguing like this. Sachi—sleep in Pallavi's room for the night."

"What?" They didn't think Priyanka and I could sleep in the same room? "I don't need to—"

"That is *enough*!" My mother's nostrils were fully flared. "Go right now, and go to sleep. Priyanka, when you are done with your homework, you must go to sleep immediately. No Internet, no telephone."

"Yes, Ma." Priyanka left the table, ducking her head. I glared at her. Even at a time like this, she had to be the perfect daughter.

"And Sachi," my father informed me, "we will write your teacher a letter removing you from this video class. Your mother and I will discuss your punishment further, but you must know now that we don't want you to do anything like this ever again."

I ran to the bathroom and burst into tears. Most parents would be proud of a child who did well in school, who had hobbies. Why weren't mine?

"I don't even want to wear a strapless dress or neglect my homework," I whispered to my tear-streaked reflection. "I just want to skip Test Prep for one semester and see my friends on weekends." I buried my face in a towel.

There was a knock on the door. "Sachi?" my mother asked.

"What?" The towel muffled my voice.

"Come here."

I opened the door. I didn't care if she saw me crying.

"Beti," she said. *Daughter.* My mother opened her arms and I fell into them—I couldn't help it. "You know how we feel about your education," she said, stroking my hair. "I understand that you want to do fun things, but education is not something to compromise on."

"I know," I said into her shoulder.

"I see you concentrating on your schoolwork," she said, "just as I did. Would you want to work that hard and make a good life for yourself, just so your daughter could throw it away?"

I raised my head. "Taking Video is not throwing my life away." Video was a real subject, even if there was no test.

Without it I'd have no way to show anyone that I had a thought in my head. I'd go back to being Nicest Girl, whose friends thought they could walk all over her.

"I know you see it this way," my mother said, "but in a few years, even a few months, you will see that your father and I are right."

I had thought she had come to make me feel better, but I'd heard her say all that a million and one times. I knew what my parents wanted for me, and everything my parents had given up for me and Priyanka and Pallavi. Still, it wasn't like we had asked them to do it. Were the schools really so much better in Manhattan than they were in Queens? And what if I would have been happier playing kick the can in front of Nani's house, instead of stranded in our neighborhood with only homework and unpaid babysitting to keep me company—where none of my classmates lived and the nearest playground was ten blocks away? Suddenly I felt too overwhelmed to argue.

"I'm tired," I said, my voice sounding thin as a crack. "May I go to bed?"

"Of course." My mother kissed me and left.

I slunk into Pallavi's room, where my little sister was sprawled out asleep above her blankets, and cried in the child-size chair in the corner.

"Mr. Phillips?" He was facing me but looking at the computer screen, a bagel in his hand. I wasn't sure if he saw me or not.

He stuck his head around the computer. "Sachi. Good." He put the bagel on its tinfoil wrapper. "Did Ms. Avery send you?"

My parents had called Ms. Avery? I couldn't believe it! And what was the note—some kind of test to see if I'd obey them? "Ms. Avery wasn't in homeroom today," I told Mr. Phillips. "I haven't even seen her."

"Hmm . . . hold on a second." He picked up the phone and punched in some numbers. "Yeah, hi again, it's Brian. I've got Sachi up here now." He took a bite of his bagel and chewed as he listened. "Oh. Okay. Sure. Yes, and call you back. Will do." He hung up.

What?

"So," he said, "can you tell me about what you did on the *Victim/Victorious* video?"

I had not been expecting that at all. "Um . . . I helped Marina film it. We were partners . . . ?"

His eyes, as dark as my own, were steady on mine. "Did you edit it with her outside school?"

Why would I do that? I wondered. "No," I said. "We didn't

even really edit together *in* school. Was I supposed to help her more?"

"So you don't know anything about this business with Rachel Winter?"

"She was in the scene Marina filmed . . . I'm not sure what you mean."

He shook his head. "We're just trying to see . . . what's going on."

"Okay." What was going on?

"You can go back to homeroom," he said, and picked up his bagel again.

"Um." I wondered if he'd forgotten that I was the one who had come to him. "I need to give you something."

He tore the bagel away from his mouth. "Oh, sorry, right. Let's see." He wiped some cream cheese off his fingers and held out his hand. I passed him the letter, already sad for what he would say.

He read. "Hunh," he said. "Oh, wow. Hunh."

What did it say? And why "Oh, wow"? Watching him was making me squirm, so I looked over at the laminated instruction sheets on the walls. I'd almost memorized them, down to the marker colors. And the posters—I loved the one of the women directors looking tough, with the big letters that said DIRECT THIS. Would I ever set foot in the video lab again? Even the posters of movies I hadn't seen felt as familiar as my own wallpaper. The video class felt more like home than home did.

"Well," he said when he was done reading, "that's too bad."

My insides unknotted a little. He wasn't mad. I guessed my parents hadn't written, *Sachi has lied to you and us and is a terrible person.*

He felt around the computer for a pen, scribbled something on the letter, and handed it back to me. I glanced down and saw that he'd written his signature on a typed line. How sneaky! If I hadn't shown him the letter, I wouldn't have known I was supposed to give it back to them signed. How humiliating, to have parents who knew more tricks than I did.

He leaned back in his chair. "I guess your parents care a lot about where you go to high school?"

Talk about stating the obvious. "Yeah."

He picked up his bagel. "My parents were like that too."

"Oh." A teacher had never told me something about his personal life before! Was this what I would miss, dropping out of Video? I couldn't stand it.

"They didn't want me to become a filmmaker," he continued. "Every time I came home, they'd tell me, 'The world needs black doctors, not black directors.' But I stuck to my guns, and I won some awards for my short films, and finally they're starting to soften up."

"Oh. That's great." Were there any awards for people my age? Maybe if I won an award, my parents would change their minds too.

"So keep trying," he said, pulling his chair up to the computer. "I know you will."

I swallowed hard so I wouldn't cry. Sometimes when people were nice, it made me sadder than if they were mean. "Thanks."

MARINA'S LITTLE BLACK BOOK,
Entry #13

* Most Annoying and Unexpected Visitors:
Mr. and Mrs. Ling
Of all the people I did not feel like seeing today . . .
yikes.
* Most Annoying Mother:
You know this one. Ugh. No comment.
* ~~Biggest~~
* ~~Worst~~
Forget it.

Of all the things that were annoying me that morning, my sweater was numero uno. I'd thought the white cashmere had been such an excellent, chic choice. *Check me, guys. I'm glowing bright and you can't stop me.* I hadn't thought about the fact that the weave was too thin for early November, especially since my hair had gotten wet on the walk down the block, so I was spending the day shivering, which, unfortunately, gave people the impression that I actually gave a woo.

They were all such drama queens! I couldn't believe I'd ever been friends with any of them. Madison and Chelsea, pulling at each other's sleeves and whispering as I passed them on the way to English. Rachel marching toward me with her head held high, pretending she didn't see me before social studies. What-ever. She obviously hadn't been in a popular group long enough to know that no one *truly* popular ever really stayed down. I just had to wait it out long enough, or figure out how to bounce myself back to the top.

In the middle of third period, math for almost dummies, and a quiz I had completely forgotten about, Mrs. Ramirez's classroom phone rang.

Everybody went, "Ooh." A phone call usually meant someone was going to the office.

In front of me someone giggled. I looked up to see the two girls who sat in the next row looking at me as if to say, *It's for you.*

"Yes?" How dare they? I didn't even know their names. "Do you need something?"

But I had barely gotten the words out before I realized that Mrs. Ramirez was walking over to me, then bending

Jessica Leader

down so low, her knees cracked. "Marina." She whispered it so loud, I was sure everybody could hear. "Ms. Avery wants to see you."

One of the girls in front of me snickered into her hand.

My skin crawled with goose bumps. Rachel had told on me. She'd told the school about a video she wasn't even supposed to watch, and I was getting hauled up to the Head of House when this was all her fault. Hers.

"You can finish the quiz at lunch," Mrs. Ramirez added.

Gee, thanks for that bit of icing on the cake.

I threw my stuff into my backpack and walked out of the room without even looking at a single one of them. Stupid plebes.

The halls were empty enough that I could warm my arms on my way to Ms. Avery's without worrying what I looked like. Still, I made sure to stop once I turned the corner to the offices, because I needed to stay cold enough to look a little pathetic. I could play it just like I had with the poll: It was a mistake, I didn't think about my actions, I'm sorry. I'd watched Angelica beg enough to work the puppy-dog eyes. I'd be in and out of there in five minutes, then spend the rest of the period in the bathroom with my iPhone. No math quiz for me today, thank you very much.

When I got to Ms. Avery's office, two grown-ups in

coats and umbrellas had already beaten me to it. Yes! Guess I'd have to come back later. But then they turned, and—

"Oh, hi." It was Mr. and Mrs. Ling! What were they—

Oh, Lord. Addie was standing in front of them, her face red and puffy like she had been crying. Ms. Avery had called them all here too.

"Hello, Marina," said Addie's dad. I always thought he and Addie looked alike: the same shiny black hair, although his was a comb-over. He was short like Addie, and mostly bald, with the same kind of squishy pink skin. Usually I liked him, but today he did not look happy to see me. Addie's stepmom, taller and wearing a brown pantsuit, only looked at me and nodded, her arm curled tightly around—

Oh my God. I knew that yellow sticker. It was Jake's laptop.

Ms. Avery was going to make me show everybody the video.

My breakfast seemed to be rushing up to my throat.

"Marina," said an angry voice. I looked toward the stairs to see my mother stalking over to me, her high heels clonking against the checkered linoleum.

"Hi," I said, and rubbed my arms. The door to the stairs had brought a burst of cold.

She bent her head toward mine, her perfume burning my

nose. "I cannot believe I am talking to Ms. Avery again. This has got to stop." Then she straightened up and nodded at Addie's dad and stepmom. "Hello."

"Hello." Mrs. Ling's arms remained folded.

Mr. Ling nodded back. "Hello."

I turned back to my mom. "Where's Dad?"

"At work." Her lips were a tight line. "I talked to him before I came here. This did not happen at a convenient time."

Well, excuse me. I wasn't in charge of the Yell at Marina Social Calendar. In fact, I'd be just as happy if we could skip this event and go back to our regularly scheduled program.

"Hi there."

Ms. Avery was standing in her doorway, her long, blue teacher sweater dangling as she reached out to shake everybody's hands. "Thank you all for coming on such short notice," she said. "Why don't you come in?"

We filed in and took our places at the chairs laid out in front of her desk—Mr. Ling, Addie, Mrs. Ling, my mom, me. When Rachel and I had been in here to talk about the poll—which seemed like ages ago—there had been only two chairs. Maybe Ms. Avery kept some hidden for when kids got in serious trouble, which I guessed this was. Oh, joy.

"So." Ms. Avery inched her chair up to her cluttered desk, her dirty-blond curls shuddering with each scoot. "As you know, I got a call this morning from a very upset parent. She said that Marina and Addie had made a damaging video about her daughter."

Damaging?

"Of course," she said, "when I hear about something like this, it is my job to investigate, which is why I'm grateful that you brought the video. I assume that's it?" She nodded toward Mrs. Ling, who was resting the laptop on her knees.

"Yes," said Mrs. Ling, her lips all pinched, "and I don't think my stepson will appreciate that I've taken it from his room. I guess Marina and Addie used a disc that they couldn't eject."

Not that I'd had any real hope for something to happen between me and Jake, but I was pretty sure having his laptop kidnapped would not speed up the process of him becoming my hot older boyfriend.

"I'd like to say something, if you don't mind." Mr. Ling's collar was too tight for his neck, and you could totally tell where Addie got her plebeness from. "We've just been talking to Addie here, and she assures us that she was not the instigator of this project. She said that Marina started it all and tried to get her involved so she could"—he looked at Addie—"use Jake's sound effects CD, was that it?"

Sniffling, Addie nodded. Was she auditioning for an acting award?

"Addie is not the kind of girl to make a cruel video," Addie's stepmother put in. "I hope you know that. She gets good grades—she cleans her room. She's never been in trouble a day in her life. This is not the kind of thing she'd be involved in."

She cleans her room? Oh, yeah, like that had anything to do with anything.

"Marina?" asked Ms. Avery. Three heads swiveled toward me. "Is this true, what Mrs. Ling says?"

She did *not* just put me on the spot. Beside me, my mother was breathing through her nose. Loudly.

What was I supposed to do? In front of Addie's parents, say, *Your daughter is a total follower who would do anything if she thought it meant people would like her, plus she never said for absolute sure that she didn't want to do it?* That wouldn't get me anywhere except deeper on Mrs. Ling's List of Poo. From the looks on their faces—frowny, sniffly, and murderous— they were probably going to slam me no matter what I did. I might as well just get it over with.

"Yeah, it wasn't her idea," I said. "It was mine."

Mrs. Ling gave a short nod. "You see?" she told Ms. Avery. "I think this was just a misunderstanding."

Not that I expected a medal, but I at least thought

someone might have thanked me for sticking up for Addie. I guess everybody was too busy thinking about themselves.

"You're sure, Marina?" Ms. Avery asked me, her thin eyebrows arched high on her forehead. "I don't want you to feel pressured to say anything here."

Oh, right! "No, I'm sure," I said. "It really wasn't Addie."

Big exhale from the mom on my right. Addie blinked, and tears ran down both sides of her face. Oscar! Oscar!

Ms. Avery smoothed a stack of papers on her desk. "I suppose I won't need you in here much longer," she told the Lings, "but Addie, I do want to know how it was that the video ended up at your house, in your computer."

Her cute older brother's computer, I thought, but didn't say anything. And I couldn't even deal with listening to their conversation about resisting peer pressure and speaking up about what you knew was wrong. If Addie was just going to nod and say "Yes" to everything Ms. Avery told her, didn't that show she was still a follower, and that she should get in just as much trouble as I did?

Eventually, after Ms. Avery swore she'd get Jake's laptop back as soon as possible, the Lings got up to leave. Mrs. Ling shot my mom a nasty look, and my mom pretended to cough—then it was just the Glasses, the Avery, and the laptop. I shivered again—this time, not from cold.

Jessica Leader

"So, Marina," said Ms. Avery, sitting back down, "I think we need to see this video."

Yeah? Because my thought was that we didn't.

"Now I'd like to say something," my mother put in. "I talked about it with my husband, and he said that if the video is on another student's laptop, there may be no proof that it was done for a school project, which means that it's not under the school's purview of discipline."

I didn't know what that meant, but from the look on Ms. A.'s face, it probably translated into something like this: *Busted.*

"My impression from the Winters is that it's very strong material," said Ms. Avery, and somehow I had the feeling that it wasn't the same kind of *strong* that got your work posted in the hallways. "And the assistant principal is concerned that it may constitute harassment."

"The video isn't finished," I broke in. "I was going to take stuff out. I know it's not, like, the nicest video on the planet, and I'm sorry that Rachel found it, but we weren't going to show that version to people. Addie and I were just playing around."

My mother and Ms. Avery started arguing about what was school equipment and what was harassment. Even though I knew some of the vocab from *Law & Order*, I gave up trying to figure out what they meant and stared at Jake's stickers. What *was* Skate Wax? And what was Siren Virus? A band? I'd have to play around on Google.

I did look up when I heard the word "consequences." What kind of consequences? I didn't think they could expel me for making a video. Would they suspend me? Woo-hoo—vacation! Even if my mom made me do something awful with the time, it would be better than hanging around in Plebeland. And hey, if they did expel me, Jane Jacobs was the only good public school in the neighborhood, so they'd have to send me to private, and all my dreams would come true. Not that I wanted Rachel to win, but I sort of wanted to tell my mom not to bother fighting.

My mother's irritated voice brought me back to earth. "All right, all right," she said, "we'll watch the video." She crossed her arms and looked to the side as if to say, *This woman is an idiot.*

"Marina, I'm not very good at finding files on my own computer, let alone a student's." Ms. Avery smiled at my mom like it was some joke between them, but I doubt she smiled back. "Can you show us the video?"

The laptop hovered in her hand, half-open, like jaws about to bite. I wanted to ask, *Do I have to?* But I knew what the answer would be.

I took the laptop from her—so heavy, it bent my wrist back—and pressed the "power" button. With the DVD stuck in there, the computer took forever to wake up, but finally it blinked its way to "on." And then, since I had no other choice, I put the laptop on the desk and pressed "play." The screen went dark, the letters faded in, all the same things I had seen millions—no, trillions—of times.

Maybe it was the difference of seeing it a few feet away from my face, or maybe it was because I had taken two days off from editing, but for whatever reason, the video looked better than usual. Yeah, there were the barfing noises, which I totally didn't need, but the pan of Rachel's outfit looked just like the way they panned on TV, and even though the sound was kind of tinny without speakers, there was no dead air—people were talking every second. I wished I could play with the light meter, because the glare off the shades was so bright, it was painful to look at. But even with that—wow. I was actually kind of proud of myself.

The sound faded out, and the screen changed to the first scene from the credits, frozen with the "play" triangle on top of it. Ms. Avery had her eyebrows raised as if to say, *Well?* But my mom was just sitting there, staring at the keyboard. Wasn't anybody going to say anything?

"Well," my mother said finally, "obviously this is in questionable taste."

Hey!

"And you can be certain that we will have a long talk with Marina when we get home."

Ugh.

"I can see why the Winters are upset, and we will make sure Marina gives them a *full* apology."

What, compared to a half apology?

"She will also be apologizing to the video teacher and yourself." The way my mother said it, I could tell she was really telling me, not Ms. Avery.

"But there's no proof that Marina planned to show this around," she continued, "and I can tell that many of the photos were taken in these girls' homes, not on school property, or using school equipment, so I think that answers the questions of the assistant principal. Still, I do want you to rest assured that nothing like this will ever happen again."

Oh, really? Because the way I saw it, Rachel still had something coming to her.

"I'll be discussing this further with the assistant principal," said Ms. Avery. "In the meantime, Marina, I want to be clear." She leaned across her desk and stared me down.

"The video you made is unacceptable, and you will no longer have a place in Mr. Phillips's video class."

Oh. Well, whatever. I should have expected that.

"In addition," said Ms. Avery, "this type of behavior has to stop now. Not with the next incident, or the one after that. No more videos or websites that tell people what you secretly think of them, or not-so-secretly think. I don't even want to hear about any gossiping. You need to turn over a new leaf—a new, positive direction for the year—and you'll start that with a week of detention, where you will spend some serious time thinking about what you did."

More detention? That office had no windows. Fifteen minutes in there after school and you forgot what your life was like. But hey, it wasn't like I could do anything to change their minds. Would they let me go now?

"I also want to ask . . ." Ms. Avery scooched in closer. "Marina, this is not the first time this year you've been called in for an incident involving Rachel. The online poll, the vocabulary test . . ."

Was I supposed to say something? "Uh-hunh?"

Ms. Avery continued, "There's a real history there, and probably some strong feelings on both sides, and I think it's worth talking about: What were you trying to accomplish when you did this? Aren't you and Rachel friends?"

I shrugged. "I guess."

"Did you two have a fight?"

Fight? "No." More like *war*.

"She's always been like this," my mother burst in.

"Like . . . ?" Ms. Avery seemed to want her to say more.

I held my breath. Like what? An evil brat?

"Intense," my mother said. "Ever since she was born. Her reactions to things . . ." My mother shook her head.

Intense? What was *that?* I wasn't intense. I was just mad because things were the way they were. Stupid. Wannabe-like. Plebeish. Squeegee. People shouldn't have to take all that. They should do something about it. Maybe some people were happy to sit back and watch it happen, but just because I wasn't didn't mean I was intense.

I couldn't believe my mother would say something dumb like that to Ms. Avery, so I pulled an Addie. As Ms. Avery talked about detention and apology notes, I nodded like I cared so the meeting would end fast. The video was my property, and they had no right to look at it or tell me I was bad or anything. And I would make sure to get it back.

The meeting with Ms. Avery lasted through all of math, and next up was lunch. I waited at my locker until I saw Sachi at hers, then walked slowly to where she stood, her olive green sweater practically blending in with the lockers. Those two friends of hers started coming toward her, their arms linked together oh-so-cute, until they saw me and swiveled back toward the stairs. Well, excuse me. Not like I wanted to talk to them, either.

Sachi, who was spinning her locker combination, hadn't seen any of this. I licked my lips and came up beside her. "Hey."

She looked up at me, then pulled down on her lock, hard. "Hi."

If anyone could say "I hate you" with a lock pull, she had just done it. Had the other night really been that bad? Okay, maybe she had been jealous about the Bar Mitzvah, but that was the weekend—get over it. "Can I ask you something?"

She curled her backpack around to her front and unzipped. "I guess."

"So . . ." I decided to dive right in. "I basically got kicked out of Video because someone didn't like the video I was making, and that's actually great for you, because now you can do your video on your own. But I was wondering: Could you maybe get my video back for me? I did all that stuff on it, and I sort of feel like it's mine, so . . . do you mind? Like, next time you're up there, you could just burn a copy for me? I can give you a blank CD if you need one."

The words came out so quickly that when I was done, I wasn't sure they made sense. Especially with the way Sachi was staring at me.

"Wait," she said, "why did you get kicked out?"

I should have known she would ask. "It's just this stupid thing with one of my friends," I said, stumbling as some squeegee knocked into me. "They thought I was trying to make them look bad . . . it was just a big misunderstanding, but, yeah. I'm out."

Sachi turned back to her bag, sliding out the textbooks and workbooks and placing them on her shiny little shelf. "Wow."

What was that supposed to mean? "Yeah. So, I mean, do you think you could do that? Help me get my video?"

Her hand paused on the shelf, and then she zipped up and said briskly, "I'm not in Video anymore either."

"What?" I thought of something horrible. "Mr. Phillips didn't think you had anything to do with *my* video, did he?" Why hadn't Ms. Avery asked me before kicking Sachi out? "Do you need me to go talk to Ms. Avery? Because I totally will." Not that I wanted to go back in there, but that wasn't right. Sachi had had nothing to do with it.

"What? No, it's not about—" She turned to face me. "My parents didn't know I was in Video. When *you* came over the other night, they found out, and now I can't be in the class anymore." She shoved her backpack into her locker, smushing it down to make it fit.

"Oh my God." They really *were* strict! "Wow. I had no idea."

She pulled the lock off the shelf and stuck it through the loop. "I'm not saying you did."

Something in her voice made me take a step back. "I mean, if I had known, I never would have shown up like that."

She snapped her lock shut. "Whatever," she said, and headed for the stairs. I followed her, wondering if I should say something else, but she was so mad, I didn't think she wanted to talk about it.

We were pretty much the only people on the stairs, and it was creepy. Above us a door creaked and slammed, and I heard every clack of my flats against the floor below. By the time we'd gone down an entire flight without talking, I felt like I had to say something.

"How weird is it that we both got kicked out in the same week?" I said. "I mean, who gets kicked out of an after-school activity?" It was almost funny.

Sachi just kept walking. Okay, I could see how she didn't think it was funny.

"But wait," I said, getting a genius idea as we opened the door to the basement, "this could totally work. Because I bet you want your footage too, right? I'm sure Mr. Phillips isn't mad at *you*. Maybe you could get yours, and you could get mine, too." I could not deal with the idea of kissing my video good-bye. "You know there's editing software on the homeroom computers, right? Not as good as the stuff in the video lab, but better than nothing. So you could work on your video." Maybe that would make her want to do it.

Sachi didn't say anything until we got to the lunch line. "You still want me to get your video?" she asked, plucking a tray from the pile.

"Um . . ." She didn't get me a tray the way my friends always did, so I stepped around her and took my own. "Yeah?"

Her hands were almost a blur as she grabbed fork, knife, and spoon. "I'm not in Video because you came over to my house without asking," she said, "and now you're asking me to get something that was so bad, you got kicked out of class?"

Whoa. Why was everything today such a drama? "I know you're upset because you got kicked out," I said, "but don't take it out on me. You didn't exactly tell me you were keeping it a secret from your family."

She turned on me, her face all twisted. "Of course you couldn't have known," she said. "But you could have at least said you were sorry!"

I felt myself flinch. She was right. I hadn't said I was sorry.

I couldn't look at her, so I slid my eyes toward the floor. Her sweater had a little hole near the seam, which for some reason made me think of her crowded apartment, and all the dishes she'd had to carry, and—

"But no," Sachi continued. "Of course you didn't apologize. You're just too—wrapped up in everything." She thumped her tray on the ledge. "Do you have any veggie burgers left?" She practically shouted at the lunch lady.

Sachi breathed out through her nose. "Then I'll have carrots."

The lunch lady ran her spoon once, twice, three times whapped the container. The water was a cloudy green, with pools of oil floating on the surface. We'd come so late, there were only a few carrots left.

"I'm sorry," the lunch lady told Sachi, handing the tray back. "We didn't know anybody else was coming down, so we gave most of it away."

Sachi stared at the tiny orange pile. "Thanks," she said quietly. And maybe it was the fact that her entire lunch was just a few soggy circles, or the way she looked like she never had any fun in her life, or knowing that someone I hadn't even meant to hate me now hated me anyway, but I knew I couldn't stand there another second. I mumbled, "I'll see you later," threw my tray into the trash, and headed for the bathroom, where, for the first time all school year, I burst into tears.

Jessica Leader

SACHI'S VIDEO NIGHTMARE #14.0

INTERIOR. JANE JACOBS MIDDLE SCHOOL
CAFETERIA—DAY

Sachi and Marina stand on the lunch line.

>   SACHI
>   (furiously)
>   Of course you couldn't have known!
>   But you could have at least said
>   you were sorry!

>   MARINA
>   Why would I apologize to
>   you? You're nothing.

Sachi bursts into angry tears.

"Sachi!" Across the lunch table, Flora and Lainey were giggling.

I snapped to attention. "What?" My heart was still hammering from what had just happened with Marina.

"We were just wondering what happened to your lunch." Lainey took a bite of her hot dog. "Did you eat it on line?"

I looked down at the puddle of carrot water. "Oh. No. They ran out of veggie burgers."

"Oh, that stinks," Lainey said sympathetically. She knew I didn't eat beef. "Do you want some of my hot dog roll?"

I shook my head. I didn't like to eat anything that had even touched red meat.

"Sachi." Flora leaned across the table, looking even more dramatic than usual. "Did you hear about Marina's video?"

Still this? "Not really." I wiped my mouth. "What happened?"

"Trouble city," said Flora. She pushed back a runaway hair, her hand covered in sparkly plastic rings. In between bites of hot dog, which I truly could not look at, she told me about the mean video Marina had made about Rachel Winter. "People were mean to Marina in math," she added, "and I say, good. She's been terrorizing everybody for years. She'd better learn her lesson."

I wished I had something to concentrate on besides my tiny pile of carrots, because I could hardly look at either of them. Marina had had a perfectly good chance to be in Video, and she'd ruined it! Why did I have to be the one stuck with her? If I'd worked with anyone else, I would still have been in class, making a perfectly fine video, and my parents wouldn't be ashamed of me.

"What's wrong?" Lainey asked. "I thought you'd be glad that you don't have to work with her anymore."

"Oh, yeah." I peeled open my water. "I am."

"Sachi probably feels sorry for Marina." Flora tipped back her milk carton.

"No, I *don't*." Even to me, I sounded sour. "I'm happy." Darn—I should have said that when they'd told me. I wasn't even *in* Video anymore, and I still had to keep track of all my lies! Who else in the school had to do that all the time? I loved my parents, but sometimes I wished I had been born into a different family.

The bell rang, and the cafeteria thundered with people pushing back their chairs.

"Ding-dong, the witch is dead," said Flora as we headed over to the conveyor belt. She folded her tray into quarters and threw it toward the trash can. "Score!"

My aim was terrible, so instead of folding my tray, I waited behind the hordes for my turn at the trash. But then I thought, *Why wait?* Not to play Styro-basketball, but to do what Marina wanted to do herself: get my video from Mr. Phillips and finish it on my own. He hadn't said anything about my lying. How much did he know?

I set my tray on a nearby table, pulled my parents' envelope out of my back pocket, unfolded the letter, and read.

Dear Mr. Phillips,

Due to an unforeseen change, we feel it is important that Sachi take Test Preparation instead of Video Elective. We apologize for the inconvenience and express our gratitude for your teaching her.

Sincerely,
Tanish Parikh

I shoved the letter back into the envelope. Thank heaven for keeping your business from strangers—they hadn't told him what I'd done. Marina was right: The teachers wouldn't be mad at me. Mr. Phillips would give me my DVD. Ms. Avery, who sometimes let me work on the computer during lunch, would let me edit. For once, things could go as I wanted them to.

As I threw my tray into the trash with a flourish, I thought, *Bye-bye, Old Sachi. Hello, video maker.*

MARINA'S LITTLE BLACK BOOK, Entry #15

* Most Annoying Silent Treatment: Rachel Winter
Grabbing people and whispering every time I walk
by is not that interesting. I'm just saying.
* Least Convincing I-Didn't-See-You Look: Addie Ling
When you sit across from me and refuse to look at
me, you might as well be looking at me.
* Most Prissy: Elizabeth Ellis
Argh. You are even too annoying to write about.
* Biggest Worry: Sachi Parikh
Amazing? Pathetic? True.

If I'd hated school before the whole Rachel thing, it was even worse with no one talking to me. It was like they thought I cared.

After Saturday, I'd unfriended all my frenemies and starting messaging the Marlowe kids between classes, so I was really not in need of the kids in Plebeland. There was just one thing that was bothering me, though, and instead of going down to lunch on Tuesday for day two of texting under the table, I waited for her at her locker.

And waited.

And waited.

Mrs. Ramirez, locking her classroom door, asked me what I was doing there. "You're not supposed to be upstairs during lunch without permission."

What was I going to do, steal computer mice? "I'm just getting something from my purse."

"Make it quick, then."

I nodded.

As soon as she was gone, I hid out in the bathroom, cracking the door open to peek when I thought I heard footsteps. Had I just missed Sachi? I swear, she hadn't gone to her locker. I'd seen her in homeroom, but had she gone home sick?

I was just about to head down to lunch, hoping that there was more left than a few slimy vegetables, when I heard someone walking, and peeked. Medium-dark jeans, turquoise shirt, black hair—it was her! It was Sachi, carrying a lunch tray. I pulled the door all the way open and stepped into the hall. Seeing me, she stopped, then moved closer to the lockers, her eyes on the floor.

"Hi." I said it quietly. "Can I talk to you?"

Sachi looked around like she wanted someone to save her. "I guess so. I'm supposed to be in Ms. Avery's room, so . . ."

"Sure." We walked down the hall. Ms. Avery's room was unlocked, and the room was empty, but I guessed if you were Head of House, you could break a few rules, especially if Sachi was the one you were breaking them for. We sat at desks across the aisle from each other. I waited until she put her napkin on her lap to talk. At least she had something to eat today—pizza and corn. I tried to ignore the rumbles in my stomach.

"So," I said, "I just wanted to say that I'm sorry about this weekend. I shouldn't have just thought it would be okay for me to come over. And I'm sorry I didn't say I was sorry yesterday. That was . . . dumb. And . . ." I took a deep breath. "I'm really sorry you're not in Video anymore because of me." Oh God—I wasn't going to cry again, was I? "That stinks."

She looked into her lap. "Thanks."

Neither of us said anything for a moment. She picked up her fork. "I'm sorry I yelled at you yesterday," she said, and took a bite of pizza.

"Oh God, no," I said, "I totally deserved it."

She shook her head slowly. "No. You didn't."

"Oh." I could see why people had voted her Nicest Girl. "Thanks."

She took another bite of pizza. Oh. I kind of liked the school's pizza. . . .

"So are you, like, helping Ms. Avery with something?" I asked. It was weird to be in a classroom with only one other person. Especially the way the sun was coming through the windows, all hot and roasty—I felt like I was in one of those movies where the world had ended and there was only one survivor. Or two.

"I'm . . . yeah, I'm sort of helping her," Sachi said, wiping her mouth.

"Something fun?" Not that I wanted to help a teacher, and especially not Ms. Avery, yuck—but at that moment I didn't feel like going down to the lunchroom. It was nice to have a break from people.

Sachi sighed. "Okay, I'm doing what you suggested. I'm working on my video."

"Wow!" I hadn't expected that. "You got your disc from Mr. Phillips?"

She nodded, taking a sip of milk.

"Cool," I said. "Can I see?"

She gave me a suspicious look. "Why?"

That one word seriously felt like a stab in the heart. What did she think I was going to do? "Just to see it," I said. "I mean, we were supposed to be partners, and you saw my video, but I never saw yours, so . . . I'm curious."

She chased the corn around on her tray. "I don't know," she said.

I stood up. "I should get some lunch," I said, and pushed in my chair and headed toward the door.

"Wait," she said. As I turned around, the sun hit me in the eye. "I didn't mean to make you feel bad."

I shrugged. "If you don't want to, you don't want to."

"No, it's just . . . the interviews aren't so great right now. I want to film some other ones. I'm not sure when or anything, but . . ."

I stepped toward her so I could stand in the shade. "It's fine," I said. "I get it." Remembering how nervous I'd felt before showing Addie my video, I really did understand.

"It's not because I'm mad," she protested, and I realized she thought *I get it* meant *Thanks a lot.* "Really . . . it's just— the interviews I did turned out kind of weird."

"What were you interviewing people about again?" I knew it had something to do with *Victim/Victorious*, but I couldn't remember what.

She squinched up her face. "Um . . . how people know

what to wear? Like, how they know what's cool, or different, or . . ."

"Oh, wow," I said. "That sounds cool."

She hunched her shoulders, like she thought I was making fun of her.

"Seriously," I said. "That's, like, really interesting."

She shook her head. "I wish it was. I just—no one really had an answer."

I leaned against a desk. "It's not like there's one answer. I mean, people just go into stores and look at magazines and wear what other people are wearing, but it's not like there's one way. You sort of just . . . know. You figure it out."

"But there are so many things in stores and magazines," Sachi protested. "Nobody is wearing those pants with the big pockets in the window of the Gap, but everybody is wearing those scarves."

"That's because those pants are butt-ugly!" I laughed.

"Yeah, but why does everybody agree?" Sachi leaned her elbows on the desk. "Or, okay, there are some things that are—unusual, but people act like they're cool, and then there are some things that maybe only one person wears, and everybody agrees it's not cool, and then they kind of make fun of that person."

Wait, was she making a video about Rachel? What the

heck? "Look," I said, "some people just use clothes to get attention, and it's really annoying, so sometimes other people get mad."

Sachi ran her finger along the edge of her tray. "But maybe it hurts their feelings. And maybe they never did anything, and they didn't mean to try to get attention, or at least, not a bad kind of attention—"

I stood up. "Okay, I'm not trying to be mean, but you don't know what happened with me and Rachel, so I kind of wish you would just—"

"Rachel?" Sachi looked puzzled. "I wasn't talking about Rachel."

"Oh." I felt stupid. "Who were you talking about?"

"Oh . . ." She poked her corn with a fork. "Kind of, my sister. She's got this koala bear key chain, and people sort of laugh at her . . . and kind of, I was talking about my friend Lainey." She looked up at me hesitantly, like she was expecting me to get mad.

"What?" I asked. Then I got it. "Did I, um, say something to Lainey?"

"Just that you didn't like her shirt." Sachi's voice was soft.

"Oh." I tried to think of what I had said, but honestly, I didn't even remember talking to her friend. "Well, I'm sorry. That was probably . . . not that nice."

Sachi picked up her fork. "Thanks."

The shade flapped against the window as the ideas from Sachi's video raced through my head. "So what did people say in the interviews?" I asked. "They didn't say anything good?"

She broke off a piece of crust. "I don't know. Some of them, sort of."

I looked at her hopefully. "Are you sure I can't see it?"

"Aagh!" She buried her face in her hand, but she was laughing. "You're going to think it's boring. Yours was, like, really fun and cute, and mine is just people talking."

"Oh," I said. "I didn't know you thought mine was . . ." *Fun and cute,* I thought, but I didn't want to sound braggy.

She nodded. "Oh, yeah. I make up videos in my head all the time and they're not even as good as yours. I mean, I could practically hear a soundtrack to yours and everything. You know that song 'Beautiful People'?"

"I love that song!" I said. "Yeah, that would be great for the red carpet scene. Oh my gosh, I should have played it while we were shooting."

She shook her head. "You wouldn't have been able to hear it. Remember, Mr. Phillips said you had to lay that kind of soundtrack over afterward?"

"Oh, right, of course." I totally knew that. But good

thing to have a partner who actually listened in class. Well, not a partner, really. Except . . .

"Hey," I said, "I know you basically have no reason to want to work with me, like, at all, but if you wanted to work on your video together, that would be kind of fun. I wouldn't make you use my stuff—I mean, not that I could get it, anyway—but I don't know. I really like making videos, and your interviews—well. I bet they're not as stupid as you think."

"Girls!"

Sachi and I turned to see Ms. Avery standing in the doorway, a grocery bag in her hand and a frown on her face. "I don't remember giving permission for this meeting."

"Sorry!" said Sachi, her voice high. "We were just talking."

Ms. Avery walked over to her desk and plunked her bag down. "*You* have permission to be up here. Marina?" She took out one of those takeout salad containers. "I hardly think someone in your position would want to be caught somewhere she shouldn't be."

"We just ran into each other, and I needed to talk to her about my video," Sachi explained, twisting her ring. "She needed to, um, fill me in on a few things. From when we were partners."

I crossed my fingers, hoping Ms. Avery would believe it.

I didn't know how I could get in worse trouble, but I didn't want to find out.

Ms. Avery pulled off her jacket. "All right," she said, folding it over the chair, "but you probably need to get down to—uh-oh." She looked at her watch. "They're not serving lunch anymore." She didn't seem happy about this.

"I'm fine," I told her. "And I can go downstairs if you need me to." As long as I wasn't going to get in more trouble, I'd go anywhere she told me to go.

"Well, that doesn't make a lot of sense." She rooted inside her plastic bag and pulled out a couple of plastic packets. "Here, at least eat something."

"Oh. Thanks." It had taken me a second to realize she was offering them to me. I walked over to her desk to take them—tiny, hard pieces of pumpernickel. Was she giving me stale bread?

"You've never had melba toast?" Ms. Avery asked.

I shook my head.

"Melba toast is great," she declared, and sank into her chair.

Sachi giggled. I looked at her, puzzled. Was this some kind of joke? In a squeegee language I didn't understand?

"Do you want it back?" I asked. I wasn't sure why she'd give me the melba toast if it was her favorite.

"No, it's for you." She waved a hand at me as she pulled out a fork.

I opened one of the packets and took a bite. Pretty dry, but better than nothing. "Thanks," I said.

She nodded and popped open her salad box.

"Ms. Avery?" said Sachi. "We were wondering . . . maybe Marina could help me with my video."

My eyes widened. Was Sachi saying yes to me?

Ms. Avery's fork, halfway to her salad, stopped in midair. "That is a very risky idea," she said. "I'm not sure how I feel about that."

"What if we only worked on it in here, when you were in the room?" I asked. "Then you could make sure that it didn't become . . . you know . . ." I scuffed at the floor. "Bad."

Ms. Avery stabbed one, two, three times at her salad before answering. *Come on,* I thought. *I can't do anything bad if you're watching, right? And I really . . . kind of . . . need something right now.*

Ms. Avery chewed and swallowed, then said finally, "Is this something you both want?"

Sachi had twisted in her chair to look at Ms. Avery, so I couldn't see her face. All I could think was, *Please say yes.*

"I think it would be good," Sachi told Ms. Avery. "Marina's

video is really fun. Well—at least it was when she filmed it," she added in a smaller voice.

Ms. Avery gave me a knowing look over Sachi's head. "Oh, I know all about Marina's video skills," she said, and I felt a slight chill. "Sachi, you're sure about this?"

Sachi nodded.

Ms. Avery took a deep breath. "Well, if you both know what you're in for," she said.

Woo! It was a yes. It was two yesses! "We do," I said, feeling happy for the first time in days.

If only everything else weren't a complete disaster.

SACHI'S VIDEO NIGHTMARE #16.0

INTERIOR. MS. AVERY'S HOMEROOM—DAY

Sachi watches her video.

    SACHI
    Hunh. This is still just people
    talking about . . . clothes.

She stares helplessly at her computer screen.

"Fine!" Priyanka slammed the door with a grunt. "I'll fail, and it'll be *their* fault!"

My eyes popped open in the dark bedroom. My mind had been stuck in a Video Nightmare, and the slam had sent my heart racing.

"What's wrong?" I asked, hoping she didn't take my head off.

She threw herself onto the bottom bunk, and the whole bed shook. "Everything. I wanted to type my paper, but Papa said no, because I'm still being punished for your stupid video." She clicked on her reading light. "Now I have to handwrite it. It'll take forever!"

"Oh." The reading light was so bright that I had to shield my eyes. "Sorry."

"Hmmph."

"Do you want me to talk to them?" I asked.

"Oh, right." I could hear her smacking her pillow into a backrest. "Like that'll help."

From underneath my arm, I stared up at the ceiling. It was the first time she'd talked to me since Saturday night. I didn't know if she'd listen to my apology now, but I had to say it. "Priyanka," I said, "I didn't mean to get you in trouble. I'm sorry."

Her pen clicked. "See if I ever help *you* again."

Oh.

Pages rustled. Her pen scratched.

What if I needed her?

"Priyanka?"

"I'm trying to work."

"Never mind. I'm sorry. Good night."

I turned onto my side. *Never* help me? My gaze fell on the bookshelf across the room, and the picture of us from elementary school, dressed like twin dogs for Halloween. I couldn't see it well from where I lay, but I knew that if I looked closely, I'd see the dots Ma had made with her eyeliner for whiskers. We'd insisted that she match the position of the dots exactly so that people would know we were twins—never mind that Priyanka was taller and had glasses. We had been best friends.

She'd helped me then, too. In first grade, when I'd thrown up in school and felt so mortified, I couldn't remember my mother's work number, the school secretary had sent for Priyanka. She'd marched right into the office and dialed the number with the confidence of a grown-up. I might have felt grown-up sometimes, but seventh grade was only halfway through school. What about high school? What about college? Would I have to go through the rest of my life as one half of twin dogs?

Tears gathered in the corners of my eyes and rolled down the side of my face. I sniffed.

"What's wrong." Priyanka said it so impatiently, it didn't even sound like a question.

"Nothing."

Her pen scratched against the page as I fought off another sniff.

"I can't write my essay if you're crying up there," she said.

"I just . . . I don't know why you started being mean to me." My voice squeaked.

There was a light thump—a pen dropped on a notebook, maybe. "Why *I* started being mean to *you*?" she asked.

"Yeah."

"Oh, like you didn't start ignoring me when you came to Jacobs?"

"I did?" I asked in astonishment. "Like when?"

"Like, all the time." Her tone mocked me from the bottom bunk.

I racked my brains. "Really?"

"Like when you read your speech at the Thanksgiving assembly last year. I went up to you and said 'Nice job,' and your friends were there and you barely even thanked me."

"I did not!"

"Yes, you did!"

For the life of me, I didn't remember having done that. "I'm sorry," I said. "I didn't mean to." That was why she'd been mad at me? That was why we had stopped riding the bus together in the mornings?

"And your video," she said. "I told you not to do it, and now you're in trouble, and Ma and Papa are mad at us."

"I'm *sorry.*" I felt so sad and cold, and pulled my knees up to my chest. "I just didn't think they would find out."

"Why couldn't you just go along?" she asked. "Why did you have to get them all mad like that?"

The light from the bunk below threw dark shadows across the ceiling. "I didn't mean to get them mad. I just really wanted to make the video. They tell us to go along with what they want, that we'll have choices when we're older, but it's hard. And Ma didn't just do what her parents did. I mean, she came here."

"That's different," said Priyanka. "She was doing something good for the family. You're just making a video to make yourself look cool."

"I'm not," I cried. "Or if I am—well—you're the one who didn't want me to tell Ma and Papa about a boy you met this summer! Or was that 'doing something good for the family'?"

"Mohan is completely different," Priyanka said quickly.

"How?" I asked.

"Because—because—because it just *is*!"

I didn't want to make her any madder, so I just said "Okay" and stared up at the ceiling while she scribbled away in her notebook.

"I can't believe you're not telling me about it," I said. "We always promised we'd tell each other if we got a boyfriend."

"Sachi," said Priyanka, "please. I'm writing a paper."

I sighed. "I know. I just . . . you'll tell me sometime, right?"

"Maybe." Now she sounded smug. "Maybe not."

I leaned over the railing. "Oh, come on! Please? I promise I won't tell anyone."

"Girls!" Our mother's voice rang through the apartment. "It's bedtime."

"Sorry!" we called.

And then I whispered, "Tell me!"

Priyanka groaned. "You're impossible," she said. "I can't concentrate on anything in here." She started rustling around.

I bit my lip. Was she going back into the living room? I had only wanted to talk.

"I might as well just take a break," she said, and before I knew what was happening, the ladder was creaking, and she appeared at the foot of my bed, her hair loose and cascading over her shoulders. "Can I come in?" she asked.

"Sure!" She hadn't asked "Can I come in?" in years.

I scooched back so she had room to climb up, and she leaned against the wall near my feet. "Wow," she said, looking out at the room, "I haven't been up here in ages. You know, when we first got the bed, the top bunk scared me."

"Priyanka!" I had guessed that about the bunk bed, but I wanted to know about the boyfriend. "Tell me about Mohan!"

She pulled her T-shirt over her knees. "Well . . . remember the last night we were at Nani's, when Ma couldn't find me?"

"*Yes*. I had to pack Pallavi's suitcase, and she kept saying I was doing it wrong."

"So . . ." Priyanka rocked back and forth slightly. "He snuck into the courtyard to say good-bye, and—we kissed! That was when he became . . . you know . . . my boyfriend."

"Oh my gosh!" I clapped my hands to my mouth. "I can't believe it! What was it like? How did you know what to do?"

Priyanka cracked up.

"Shush!" I protested, but I was laughing too. "How else am I supposed to know? You have to tell me! Was it on the lips?"

She smiled. "Yup."

"Oh!"

Her smile deepened. "Yeah."

"Are you still going out?" I asked.

"Yeah. At least, we still e-mail. He uses a girl's screen name to write me in case they see."

"Sneaky!"

Priyanka wiggled her eyebrows. "What can I say?"

I couldn't believe it. I didn't like the way Marina and her friends divided the class into cool people and nerds, but all the same, I had pretty much thought Priyanka was a nerd. All this time, though, she'd had a boyfriend, and even gotten kissed! I felt a new respect for her. Not because it made her cool, but—she had secrets too.

"I didn't mean it before," Priyanka said suddenly.

"What?"

"About not helping you ever again."

"Oh." Tears prickled my eyes, but for a different reason than they had earlier. "Thanks."

"Why?" Priyanka sounded wary. "What's going on?"

I tried to sound normal. "What makes you think something's going on?"

"Sachi."

She said it so knowingly, I sighed. I guessed you couldn't hide too much from someone you'd shared a room with all your life.

"Marina asked if I wanted to work on the video with her outside of class," I told Priyanka, "and I said yes."

"What?" Priyanka's eyes bulged out. "On that *Victim/Victorious* thing? You're helping her with *that*?"

"No!" I said, although I couldn't believe that even Priyanka knew what Marina's video had been about. "We're working on my video."

"What? Why? And why do you have to work with *her*?" Priyanka hunched over her knees.

I pulled my blanket up to my chest. "I think it's going to be good. I had filmed all these interviews, and they didn't turn out that well, but Marina thinks she knows how to make it all work." Although before Priyanka had come in, I had been worrying about that . . .

"What's it about?" Priyanka asked.

So she wasn't going to tell? "Well," I said cautiously, not wanting her to change her mind, "have you ever noticed that people seem to think some cultures are cooler than others?"

She looked suspicious. "Yeah?"

"So, that's sort of what it's about. Like how you hear kids say 'Wassup?' like the African-American kids do, or they say 'Ojé, Mami' like the kids from the Dominican Republic. But they never say, 'Hey, Ma-ji! How's it hanging?'"

"Yo!" said Priyanka, grinning. "Namaste! Welcome!"

We giggled. The sound of footsteps came near our room. "Girls?" said my mother.

As Priyanka and I laughed silently into our hands, the footsteps padded away.

"It's true," Priyanka whispered. "Everyone listens to R&B, but Indian music, forget it."

"Not when *My Jaiphur Bride* came out," I pointed out. "That was the year everyone wanted us to dance bhangra, remember?"

Priyanka rolled her eyes. "Oh, I remember. Every few years something Indian becomes cool, and then people forget about it."

"I know!" I cried. "I want to say to them, 'Wait! I was cool last year.'"

"Hello?" said Priyanka, with a hint of Nani's accent that made me giggle. "Have you forgotten about us over here, on the other side of the globe?"

It felt so good to laugh about it! And I couldn't believe I was laughing with Priyanka. All this time, I'd wanted Lainey or Phoebe or Marina to explain to me how popularity worked, but it was Priyanka, with her koala bear key chain, who made me feel better about it.

"Who decides that stuff?" I asked. "Is there someone sitting in a room somewhere, sticking their finger on a map and saying, 'This will be the year of the Indian'?"

"Maybe. We talked about that in social studies. People need a way to make money, so they're like, 'Everyone needs to buy short skirts. . . . Okay, no more short skirts—long skirts. And now you must buy Indian clothes!'"

"Which people?" I asked.

"I don't know," said Priyanka. "The Gap."

I giggled. "Do you think the Gap will ever sell saris?"

"Oh, yes," said Priyanka, now definitely sounding like Nani. "Saris will be their number-one bestselling item."

We laughed into our hands again, then widened our eyes as we heard Ma and Papa walk down the hall, talking softly, and click their door shut. It must have been later than I thought.

"Hey," I said, "could I interview you for my video? Everything you just said—that should be in there."

Priyanka shrank back against the wall. "Who are you showing it to?" she asked.

"I don't know yet."

"I don't think so," she said. "I mean, it's kind of personal."

"But it was *good*."

She made a face.

"Will you think about it?" I asked.

She shrugged. "Okay." Then she pulled off the blanket. "We should get some sleep."

"Wait." I had to be sure of something. "Are you going to tell Ma and Papa that I'm still working on it?"

She paused for a moment on the ladder. "No," she said finally. "But if they find out, you really can't tell them I knew."

"No, of course not."

"Okay, then."

As she started to disappear from view, I sat up. "Hey," I said, "thanks."

She nodded and continued down the ladder.

<u>Sachi's Video Plan 16.1</u>

INTERIOR. MS. AVERY'S CLASSROOM—DAY

        SACHI
        Marina! I figured out what we need
        to do.

MARINA'S LITTLE BLACK BOOK, Entry #17

* Most Shocked: Marina Glass
She's so shocked, she can barely even write this.
* Still Most Wrong: Rachel Winter
No! No! I still won't say it.
* Most Annoying Idea: Sachi Parikh
You said I had good ideas. How about listening to them?

"And don't forget," Mrs. Ramirez was saying, "we have another quiz next Monday. Study hard, people."

The class groaned. The bell rang. The talking started.

"I can't believe we have another quiz."

"I know, she's so mean."

"Dude, do you know what's for lunch today?"

"It better not be taco salad. That stuff was nasty."

"Wait, I have to tell you what she said."

The voices floated into my ears whether I wanted them

to or not. I had never noticed how much people talked before. It was like they never shut up. When I had people to talk to again, I would make sure not to sound as stupid.

No chance of that now, though. I picked up my books and headed to my locker, looking straight ahead, never saying a word. But still—lunch—video time! I'd had some ideas about what to do with Sachi's interviews, but more than that, I just wanted to *talk* to somebody. Ooh, and there was Sachi at her locker! As I walked up to her, I realized I was not walking. I was bouncing.

"Hey!" I said. "Sachi," I added when she didn't turn around.

She turned around. "Oh, hi." She looked over my shoulder down the hall, then in the other direction, like she was scoping out the scene. What was that about? Weren't we going to work on the video together?

"Are you ready to get lunch?" I asked. "You know, so we can work on the video?"

She nodded—good. "I just have to get my pass from Ms. Avery." She opened her backpack and began pawing through it.

"Don't worry about it," I said. "She'll write you a new one."

"No, I got it." She pulled out a folded piece of loose-leaf paper, zipped up her bag, and closed her locker.

"Cool. Come on, let's get mine." I turned and started to walk toward Ms. Avery's room, but then I realized Sachi wasn't next to me. When I turned back, I realized she was standing with her friends.

Oops. Guess I had missed that. "See you upstairs," I told her, and waved.

She nodded. Her friends turned around and looked at me. What were *they* staring at? I hurried toward Ms. Avery's room, hoping I hadn't missed her.

It had taken me so long to track down Ms. Avery for my pass that I ran down the stairs to lunch, not wanting to waste any more time. When I threw open the door to the cafeteria, a barking laugh bonked me in the eardrums. Oh, great. Ex-friends in the house.

The menu outside the serving line said it was ravioli day, and I was hungry, but I did not need to go in there, so I backed into the corner by the stairs and waited. Rachel would get her food and then I'd get mine.

"She is so going to die," said a voice—Chelsea? Addie? "I mean, she is seriously going to die."

"Omigod, she wrote that?" That was definitely Addie. "I can't believe she wrote that."

What? Who wrote what? And who was going to die? I

crept forward so I could peek into the serving line. They were all there—Rachel, Madison, Chelsea, Addie, and Elizabeth at the end. Did "she" mean me?

Rachel and Chelsea were looking at something on Rachel's tray. I couldn't see it, but I didn't think it was ravioli. I inched closer as Chelsea picked up whatever it was, and a whole bunch of little papers fell to the ground, scattering over the brown floor tiles.

"Chelsea!" Rachel groaned. "I had those in order!"

"Sorry!" Chelsea squatted down and started picking them up. One had floated into the doorway—a scrap with turquoise. Wait a minute—was that mine? I wrote in turquoise all the time. I stepped forward and bent down to grab it.

"Rachel!" Chelsea squealed, and before I knew it, a hand with silver nails snatched the note away from me.

"Hey!" said Rachel. We stood up, face-to-face—well, eyes to nostril, because she was so grossly tall. "That belongs to me."

The way she said it made me think she was lying somehow, and through her claws I could see that the handwriting was mine. "Excuse me," I said, "it actually belongs to me." I tried not to breathe in her breath. "You seem to have a real thing for looking at stuff that isn't yours, Rachel."

She pursed her lips—maroon today, triple yuck. "It's

mine now," she said. "But soon I'm going to share it with everybody." The maroon blobs curled into an evil smile.

"What do you mean?" I looked at the Plebe Squad for clues, but their lips were zipped. "What do you mean, 'share it'?"

"Do you girls want lunch or what?" the lunch lady asked impatiently.

Rachel handed the note off to Chelsea, who tucked it into a folder and scurried off into the lunchroom, then smiled at the lunch lady. "Sorry, Melinda," said Rachel. "Can I have some ravioli, please?"

She knew the lunch lady's name? Show-off. I glanced at Elizabeth, who was still standing at the end of the line, her face completely blank.

"You might as well tell me what it is," I told Rachel. "You obviously want me to know."

Addie gave Madison a nervous look behind Rachel's back. What were they planning? Somebody should just tell me.

Rachel took her tray from the lunch lady—Melinda—with an even bigger smile than before. "The notes," she said sweetly. "Yours. About people. You seem to really want people to know what you think of them, so we're going to do you a favor and make them public."

"Hello?" Melinda waved at me over the counter, and I

realized she was talking to me. "We're going to start closing up here."

"Ravioli, please," I said, breathless like a moron, then turned back to Rachel. "Public where?" If people saw the White Pages, Volume 2—oh God. I wouldn't have a single friend in Jane Jacobs Middle School. The tomato sauce suddenly smelled overly sweet, and I didn't even want to look at the ravioli.

Rachel moved to the end of the line. "That's for me to know and you to find out. Liz-Bird, did they ever get you your cheese?"

Elizabeth shook her head.

"Poor thing," said Rachel, and put her hand lightly on Elizabeth's shoulder as she left the lunch line. She waved over her shoulder and said, "Later, Marina."

Melinda passed me back my tray. I thanked her—I think.

A different lunch lady appeared from behind the counter and handed Elizabeth a Parmesan cheese shaker, filled to the top. "Sorry you had to wait so long, sweetheart."

"That's okay," said Elizabeth. "Thanks, Evelyn."

Did everybody know the lunch ladies' names but me? When did that happen? The plebes ganging up against me—Rachel plotting to humiliate me. It was like I'd stepped into a new and horrible universe, right there on the lunch line.

"Elizabeth." I slid my tray toward her. "What is Rachel

talking about?" Even though we were right near the tomato sauce, her perfume drifted under my nose, and I tried to ignore how homesick it made me. "Is Rachel going to make a book or something out of the White Pages?" Then I realized it could be worse. "Wait—is she going to put them on the Internet?" That could not happen.

Elizabeth shook the cheese over her plate. "I'm not supposed to tell," she said.

"Bird, come on." I knew I sounded desperate, but I didn't care. "Or—whatever, it doesn't matter what it is. Can you tell her not to do it?"

"I tried." She clicked the container shut. "She won't listen. She doesn't even care that she's going to get in trouble." Elizabeth looked like she was in pain.

"When is she going to do it?" The sound of people talking in the lunchroom seemed far away and close at the same time. "Like, today?"

Elizabeth bit her lip. "I don't know. She keeps changing her mind."

That was good news, at least. "So can't you, like, *really* change her mind? Tell her to stop?"

She stepped aside so some kid who had come in through the back could get to the cheese. "I think she wants you to apologize."

"I already wrote her an apology letter! What more does she want?"

"But Ms. Avery made you write that one, right? I think she wants you to *say* you're sorry."

Ugh! It was just like when the hairdresser had burned Rachel's neck. She needed *everyone* to wear a hat at the pity party.

"She's really upset," Elizabeth said. "She's been wearing sneakers all week. It's like she's afraid people are going to make fun of her, after what you did."

I grabbed the container and shook cheese onto my pasta. "If Rachel really thinks her clothes are so great, she wouldn't care if someone else made fun of them." Apologizing would be like saying it was wrong to make fun of her clothes, and I could think whatever I wanted about them.

"But you were friends!" Elizabeth cried. "Don't you care that you made her feel bad? And now she's going to do the same thing to you. You're going to feel just as bad, and it's going to keep going on like this unless one of you stops it. People are starting to think we're crazy. Alex keeps being like, 'The girls are so moody this week,' and Crystal came up to me in rehearsal to ask me about the drama. Can't you just end it now? What is so bad about telling her you're sorry?"

"Eliza-*beth*." Chelsea had shown up at the back door of the lunch line with a pout on her face. "Rachel wants to know what's taking you so long."

Elizabeth picked up her tray. "Will you think about it?" she asked me. "Please?"

I didn't even want to say that I would.

Elizabeth's eyes were still on me as she left with Chelsea, and I could hear Chelsea's not-so-soft whisper, "What was she saying to you?"

Oh, these plebes! I couldn't stand it. Who cared about the notes—who cared what any of them thought of me? I had one thing to do—well, two: check online about applying to Marlowe and work on the video with Sachi. I could do both upstairs, so I showed the teacher on duty my note from Ms. Avery and ran upstairs as fast as I could without spilling tomato sauce on my sweater.

When I got upstairs, Ms. Avery and Sachi were talking about some show I hadn't seen—was Citizen Kane a person or a movie? I couldn't figure it out—so I got to eat my ravioli in peace. It took me three raviolis to realize that the whole thing was way too salty, and to look down and see that I'd covered it with so much cheese, I could barely even see the pasta. I took a big gulp of water, but my mouth still felt hairy, and it was all Rachel's fault. If she hadn't made me mad with her stupid plan and brainwashed Elizabeth into telling me to apologize, I would have been enjoying my favorite lunch. Well, my favorite *school* lunch.

A voice came over the speaker and said, "Ms. Avery, we need you in the office."

"Oh, right." Ms. Avery sighed. "I'll be right back, girls," she said, and hurried out the door.

"Hey." Sachi pushed her lunch tray to the edge of the desk where she was sitting. "Are you okay?"

"What?" I asked. "Yeah. Why?"

She shrugged, and the cute hoops she was wearing bobbed up and down. "I don't know. You just look upset."

"I'm fine," I said. "I'm just ready to work on the video. Do you want to finish showing me your DVD?" We hadn't had time to watch it all yesterday before the bell rang.

"Yeah," she said, "and I even have some notes for another interview."

"Cool." I ate a ravioli that didn't have so much cheese on it. "With who?"

She pulled a notebook out of the bag next to her and flipped through it. "My older sister. We were talking last night, and she said all these interesting things that I want her to say on-camera."

"Hunh." The night I'd come over, her sister had mostly shot me mean looks. "What did she say?"

Sachi's eyes were still on the notebook. "Just about how so much of trends is what people decide to put in stores, and how stores only come up with new trends so we'll buy more stuff."

"Um, okay." I scraped the cheese off the next ravioli—crappy Parmesan. "But that's not really what we're talking about. I mean, yeah, there's new stuff in stores, but some people choose it better than others."

"Yeah, but don't you think it's weird that everyone agrees on things at the same time? Like, every three years people think something Indian is cool, and then it's like, 'Bhangra music is boring.'"

Who had said anything about bhangra music? And why was this turning into Marina and Sachi's Very Special Tour of the World? Focus, people—focus.

"I see what you're saying," I said, trying to let her down easy, "but I think that's too much. Remember what Mr. Phillips said—'K-I-S-S? Keep It Simple, Stupid'?" Ew, the one thing I remembered from Video had the word "kiss" in it? "Let's just keep it about trends here at school."

"But why?" asked Sachi. She pulled her hands under the desk, and I would have bet anything she was playing with her ring. "I think it's more interesting if we don't just talk about things at school. I mean, is Jacobs really that different from anyplace else?"

What, so talking about school fashions wasn't good enough? I punched my fork into the Styrofoam tray. "Lots of people care about what people wear to school," I said, making rows, then a square, then a bigger square with my punches. "If we start talking about store owners and Indian music, the video's going to be like a social studies class."

That had to get her. Squeegees never wanted to seem like squeegees. And I would not have my video be squeegee.

"Maybe," said Sachi, "but I still want to talk about why things are the way they are. I mean, that was what I wanted to do with the video in the first place."

I punched my fork in again, and it scratched through to the desk.

"We can put in the fun stuff that you shot," Sachi continued. "I can ask if Mr. Phillips will give you back your *Victim/Victorious* footage. I just want to have the other ideas in there too."

"But that's not how I thought of it!" I jammed my fork into the tray, then tried to pull it out, but I couldn't. It was stuck.

I shoved the tray across the desk. Everything was stuck!

Everybody wanted me to do what *they* wanted, all the time. Apologize—talk about random music. I was just—so—sick of it.

The sun burst into the room again, making my fork and tray glow so bright, I had to squint, and through my squint I could see that the tray looked really, really stupid. Who would put a fork in a tray? Forks were for eating with. Trays were for holding food. Anyone who would stick a fork in a tray was just too much. Too—oh God, did my mother's word just pop into my head?— intense.

And suddenly, I was sick of being that person. Why did I care if people knew the names of the lunch ladies? Why did it matter to me if Rachel became dance captain, or tried to look like a model during the school day? I couldn't stand the way Rachel was being such a drama queen, but if I wouldn't even interview the person Sachi wanted me to— Sachi, who was doing me a huge favor—I was just as bad. And even though I was starting to like Sachi, I didn't want to eat lunch with her for the rest of the school year. I wasn't even really sure my parents would want to pay for Marlowe. As Elizabeth had said, it had to stop.

"Okay," I said. "Let's do it. Let's interview your sister."

Sachi looked at me in surprise. "Really?"

"Yeah." I got up to throw away my tray. The ravioli was

inedible, and what would I eat it with, anyway? "You're right. We can ask people about music and that other stuff. Maybe they'll say something good."

She came up beside me and threw her tray on top of mine. "Okay. Great."

The hallway started buzzing with the noise of people coming upstairs. The bell hadn't rung for sixth period yet, but sometimes the teachers got so sick of us in the lunchroom, they sent us upstairs early.

"Sachi!" Her friends appeared in the doorway, looking confused.

"What are you doing here?" asked the one with the black hair. "I thought you said you were helping Ms. Avery."

"I was," said Sachi, pressing down her tray so it didn't take up the entire garbage can.

"Then where is she?"

"I'll see you later," I told Sachi, and hurried into the hall. Science was next, with Rachel and Addie, and I wanted to talk to both of them.

Jessica Leader

ANOTHER SACHI VIDEO ~~NIGHTMARE~~ LIFEMARE #18.0

INTERIOR. MS. AVERY'S HOMEROOM—DAY

Sachi stands at the door with Marina. Flora
and Lainey appear.

>   FLORA
>   Sachi! What are you doing here?
>
>   SACHI
>   I'm helping Ms. Avery.
>
>   LAINEY
>   But Sachi . . . Ms. Avery isn't
>   here. And Marina is. And we don't
>   like Marina!
>
>   MARINA
>   I am so out of here.

"I knew it!" cried Flora. "I knew you were helping her!"

I stepped back so the kids coming into the room wouldn't trample us. "What do you mean?" I asked.

"I saw you and Marina talking before," Flora said, coming toward me. "You weren't up here doing something for

Ms. Avery. You were helping Marina with her video."

I gripped the door of the coat closet.

"Sachi, you shouldn't let her do this," Lainey said, tugging on her necklace. "She's using you."

Around us, kids were yelling and tossing each other soda bottles. The room was bright and the coats smelled musty, and I started to feel sick.

"She's not using me," I said.

"Oh, come on." Flora crossed her arms. "What, you think she's going to do something nice for you afterward? You think you guys are going to become friends? You heard what she did to Rachel Winter. And that was her friend."

As always, I wished Flora would lower her voice. "You guys . . ." I took a deep breath. "I have to tell you something."

"What," said Flora, "that you and Marina are secret BFFs?"

"No." There was some kind of dirt on the floor by the closet, and I crunched it beneath my feet. "I got kicked out of Video too, and Marina and I are working on our video together."

"What?" Flora looked outraged.

"What?" said Lainey. "It's not because of her video, is it? You didn't have anything to do with that."

I shook my head.

"Folks?" The whole room stopped and looked at Ms. Avery, whose voice boomed into the room. "This is unacceptable. If I need to come late to class because I'm in a meeting, you should be mature enough to handle that. *Sit* down, take out your books, and if I see any soda in the next fifteen seconds, you will be in my office after school, stuffing envelopes."

I turned to Flora and Lainey. "Can we please talk about this later? The bell is going to ring in three minutes, and I still need to get my books for English."

"Just tell us what's going on," Flora urged.

"My classroom, my time." Ms. Avery was passing out papers and paused to whip someone's baseball cap off his head. "Doesn't matter if the bell has rung or not."

"You guys," I pleaded with Flora and Lainey. Ms. Avery was the last person I wanted to be mad at me.

"Come *on*," said Flora.

I threw my hands into the air. "Fine." I kept my voice low in the hopes that Ms. Avery wouldn't notice us at the side of the room. "My parents didn't want me to take Video, but I signed up anyway, and when they found out, they said I had to take Test Prep, so Marina and I are working on a video. Okay? It's going well and she's not using me, so can we please just go to class?"

"Wait," said Lainey, "you lied to your parents?"

"I—" I hadn't expected her to say anything about my parents, of all things. "Yeah."

"Did they freak out?"

"Well—"

Beside Lainey, Flora was shaking her head. "You're so different this year," she said.

I looked at her in surprise. "What do you mean?"

"The video about clothes? Making a video with Marina? You never would have done *that* last year."

"Girls," said Ms. Avery, "it's time for class. Sachi, we're starting. You need to take your seat."

"She's bad news, I told you!" called Alex, and the whole class laughed. Oh! Now, of all times?

"I just have to get my things," I said breathlessly, heading for the door.

"Make it quick," said Ms. Avery, who was glaring at everybody for silence.

I stalked out of the room so fast, my shins burned.

How dare Flora accuse me of changing! She was the one who was acting so different this year, pretending her parents let her do whatever she wanted, and getting obsessed with looking cool. She was the one who needed to go back to the way things were.

My heart thumped as I fought my way to my locker, Lainey and Flora following at my heels. Could I tell her that? We'd been best friends for four years, and we'd never had a fight. But if I could stand up to Marina Glass, surely I could talk to Flora.

We reached my locker. I turned around, my stomach rolling with nerves.

"Flora," I said, "I'm sorry I didn't tell you about the video, but maybe it's because you're always talking about how pathetic my life is."

"What?" cried Flora. "What are you talking about?"

"When you were like, 'Oh, Sachi can't wear this necklace,' or 'Sachi can't go downtown,' or 'Sachi can't talk to a boy.' How do you think that makes me feel? Especially when you say that in front of other people? Your parents have rules too, but I'm not telling people about them. So please don't tell other people things about me, especially if they're not even true."

Flora opened her mouth to speak and then closed it. "I was just—," she began. "I wasn't *trying* to—," she said. Then she let out a breath of air and looked at the floor. "Okay," she muttered, "I won't."

The first bell rang. I realized my heart was pounding.

"I'm sorry I'm working with someone who was mean to

you," I told Lainey. "But if it makes you feel any better, she told me she was sorry for making fun of your shirt."

"Oh." Lainey shrugged. "That's okay. Just as long as you don't make fun of it in your video."

"Of course I wouldn't!"

"I hope you're going to talk about my bicycle-chain necklace in your video," Flora put in. "Because I heard Marina saying that this year bicycle-chain necklaces are *hot.*"

I looked at Flora, about to say, "Are you *serious*?" Then I realized she was grinning, and the three of us burst out laughing.

"Sachi Parikh, Flora Jasari, and Lainey Freeman-Reese." Ms. Avery's voice echoed down the hall. "You have exactly thirty-seven seconds . . ."

"Sorry!" we cried, and ran to get our books.

MARINA'S LITTLE BLACK BOOK, ENTRY #19: A VIDEO NIGHTMARE

INTERIOR. SCIENCE LAB—DAY

    MARINA
    Rachel, I'm sorry I made that
    video.

    RACHEL
    You're sorry? Who cares? I made the
    website during lunch, and everybody
    already hates you even more.

VIDEO NIGHTMARE 19.1

    MARINA
    Rachel, I'm sorry I made that
    video.

    RACHEL
    What? I'm sorry, did somebody just
    say something? Oh, I guess it was
    just a really strong wind.

>MARINA
>Rachel, I'm sorry I made that
>video.
>
>RACHEL
>I'll show you sorry. I'll—

"Okay, everyone." Ms. Lewis's voice broke through my thoughts, and I almost jumped out of my seat. I could see what Sachi meant when she'd talked about playing videos in your head. Once you started, it was hard to stop.

"Okay," said Ms. Lewis, "time to set up for that bell-jar planting experiment you read about last night. Partners, go to the supply area and get—"

"Ms. Lewis!" Rachel called out without raising her hand. "I need to change partners! Addie and I want to be partners now."

"Oh, we want to change too!" It was that guy Noah who'd been in Video with me. "Me and Javon want to swap with Dardan and Jack."

"Guys!" Ms. Lewis held up her hand. "We're not switching lab partners today. Deal with it, and get to your stations."

"She thinks she's so cute," Rachel muttered under her breath.

I let Rachel stay at the lab table talking to Addie while I loaded up the grocery basket with supplies—plant, trowel, soil, washcloth, empty pot, and something that looked like the glass top of a cake platter. When I got back to our table and started unloading, Rachel turned around and slid her books to the side—not to help me, I was sure, but to make sure she didn't get dirt on her notebook. *When you take out the little shovel,* I told myself, *you have to say it. Okay, no—when you take out the dirt, you have to say it. Okay, right—when you put the pot on the counter . . .*

"Rachel," I blurted out, "I'm sorry about the video."

Watching me unload the basket, she snorted. "Yeah, of course you're sorry now. You just don't want me to put your White Pages notes online."

So she *was* planning to do that. Just like on the lunch line, everybody's voices got louder, and the room seemed to grow and shrink at the same time. I picked up the little plant, feeling the thin plastic baggie crinkle in my hand.

"I don't want you to post the notes," I admitted, setting the plant next to the pot. "But they kind of made me see your point about the video—that it's not, like, fun to think about everybody laughing at you. I mean, you should wear what you want to wear. And I shouldn't have made a video about it."

She looked down her nose at me. "You were going to

show people that awful video, and you dragged Addie into it. Apology *not* accepted."

Ugh! Why didn't she want to make up? Elizabeth was right: Putting up a website would only make things worse. I didn't want worse—I wanted to end the war. I grabbed the little plant and started massaging the roots, trying to loosen them up the way Ms. Lewis had shown us. What could I say to get Rachel to call it quits?

"I should warn you," I said, "I'm doing serious detention for the video. You'll probably get it too if you put up that website."

Rachel untied the soil bag. "My parents won't care."

How could I have forgotten that? "You're lucky," I said, watching her grab the trowel. "My parents are majorly mad."

She shrugged.

Okay. Should I keep telling her nice things? "Hey, did you see?" I asked. "That Hula-hoop belt you have was on *Modelicious* the other night."

She dug into the soil. "I saw."

"I guess you knew something I didn't."

Rachel dumped the soil into the pot. "I guess so."

Argh! I was getting nowhere! Did I really want to be friends with Rachel so badly that I would let her keep insulting me? This was torture!

I suddenly noticed someone giggling nearby, and looked across the lab table to see the annoying girls from my math class huddling together and whispering. "I heard there were barfing noises!" one of them said, and the other one snickered. They noticed I had heard them, and pretended to be busy filling up their pot. Next to me Rachel was doing the same thing and biting her giant lips.

Wow. I didn't know that people had heard about the video outside of our group. So that's what it would have been like, I thought, if I'd shown it: kids I didn't even know having their laughs.

I needed to try again. If Rachel posted the notes, I would just want to get back at her, and it would keep going until everyone thought we were a joke.

"If you don't like *them* laughing," I said, "wait until you're in detention. There are these eighth-grade guys in there, and every day they've been like, 'What did you do? What did you do?' And when I see them in the halls, they're like, 'She's the bad one!'"

Rachel's eyes flicked toward me. I could tell she was thinking, *Really? I don't want that.* At least that's what I hoped she was thinking.

There were no eighth-grade boys in detention. But I knew she cared about eighth-grade boys in general. And if a little story was what it took . . . "If you really want to post the notes, go ahead," I said. "I probably deserve it. I just want you to know what you're in for."

"You just need to have everything your way." She dug a hole in the soil so we could stick in the plant. "I'm so over it."

"I know," I said. "I'm trying to stop."

Rachel glanced up at me, then looked quickly back down. What was that? Was I getting through?

"Oh, fine," Rachel said, rolling her eyes. "If you need to get your way about everything . . . fine." She grabbed the plant and plunked it into the hole.

"Fine?" I watched her hands as they buried the top of the plant with dirt. "Fine, like . . . okay?"

She put the cake-top thing over our plant. "Okay."

Hallelujah!

We piled the leftover things into the shopping basket, wiped off the counter, returned our supplies, and headed over to the sinks.

"So, what was this all about, anyway?" I asked as she washed the tools. "This planting-a-tiny-little-tree thing? What are we supposed to be discovering—just how to grow a plant?"

"It's to see if plants can survive without oxygen." Rachel wiped her wet hands on a paper towel.

"Oh." I took my turn at the sink. "They can't. Duh!"

"Actually, they can." She stepped on the trash-can lever and threw away her paper towel, then kept her foot down so I could toss mine in after.

"Right," I said as we headed back to our seats. "I knew that."

As Ms. Lewis wasted what could have been an actual moment of free time by asking how our labs went, Addie scribbled frantic notes to Rachel. Was Rachel going to backstab me now—use my apology as part of her website? I was trying to think what to write to Rachel in a note of my own when Rachel looked at me and rolled her eyes. "Plebe," she mouthed, tilting her head toward Addie with a mournful expression.

I laughed into my hand, but part of me thought, *Ouch*. Addie had probably been nice to Rachel the whole time since the Bar Mitzvah, and the minute we made up, Rachel was slamming her? I would never do that to Elizabeth.

Elizabeth! She would be so happy Rachel and I had made up. She'd be my friend again, though, right? Because I had made up with Rachel? I had said bad things to Elizabeth, too, though, I knew. I needed to talk to her.

When the bell rang, Rachel, Addie, and I walked out of science together and stopped short. We'd almost walked right into Señora Blanca.

"Hola, Señorita Glass, Señorita Winter, y Señorita Ling," she said with a big smile.

"Um, hola," Rachel and I replied at the same time. The minute Señora passed us, we burst out laughing.

"Oh my God." Rachel clutched my arm. "Why does she still say hi to us? Does she not know that we hate her?"

I turned to face her at the entrance to the stairwell. "You know, Rach, it's okay to admit that you hang out with her outside of school."

"What?" Rachel cracked up. "I so do not."

"Seriously." I patted her shoulder. "I don't mind if you admit it. Just say, 'Señora Blanca is my favorite teacher.'"

"You became her fan online!"

"Only because you recommended her!"

Addie was shaking her head, smiling. "You two are nuts," she said, and all around us the plebes, the squeegees, and maybe even a few normal people were looking at us like they were thinking the same thing. Drama? Yes. But just the right amount.

SACHI'S VIDEO NIGHTMARE #20.0

INTERIOR. PARIKH APARTMENT—DAY
Sachi arrives home from school. Sachi's mom
appears from the living room, solemn.

    SACHI'S MOM
    Sachi?

    SACHI
    Yes?

    SACHI'S MOM
    We know. We know what you've been
    doing.

Sachi's face crumbles.

    SACHI'S MOM
    I honestly don't know what to do
    with you anymore.

    The familiar sound of the stair door slamming made me and Marina look at each other in dismay.

    "I can't stand it," she said, hitting "save." "We barely even come up from lunch, and bam! The period is over."

"I know."

"Why can't my parents just give me my computer back already?" she asked, ejecting the disk. "It's been two weeks."

"Yeah," I said, "but I probably couldn't come over, anyway."

She snapped the DVD into its clear purple case. "Parents suck."

I fingered the strap of my backpack. "I guess."

"You guess?" She gave me a curious look. "Hello, all you did was take a video class, and you're, like, on house arrest."

I shined the mouse light around the desktop. "Yeah . . ."

"Yeah *what?*" she asked.

"I don't know." When I held the mouse up to Nani's ring, it made the onyx reflect red. "I lied to them. And . . . I don't like lying. And I think they'd be really upset if they knew I was still doing the video."

Marina zipped up her backpack. "So you, like, actually care if they're mad at you?"

I replaced the mouse on its mat. "Yeah." Why wouldn't that bother me?

"Wow," said Marina, "that's kind of cool. I mean, that you care."

I hadn't really thought of it that way.

Kids had started coming into Ms. Avery's room, but I had something to ask Marina. "So," I said, "do you have any advice on talking to my parents? I mean, don't take this the wrong way, but you're kind of good at getting people to do things."

"Oh yeah, so good." Marina snorted.

"I'm serious."

From the way her cheeks had pinked up, I could tell my comment had pleased her. She put on her backpack. "Well, okay. So, the problem was that they wanted you to take Test Prep, but you changed the form and lied to them?"

"Yeah. And that I made Priyanka help me."

"Okay." Marina stared out the window, thinking. "What do you think would happen if you just told your mom you were making a video?"

I moved to the side so someone could grab a jacket off the desk. "Just *told* her?" I didn't see the plan in that.

"Yeah. Here, walk me to my locker."

The bell hadn't rung yet, so I stood up. "Why should they let me?"

"I don't know." We headed into the hall, where the sound of lockers slamming was deafening. "Why do *you* think they should let you?"

I walked slowly, trying to think despite the noise. "They always say they want me to work hard and accomplish something. I think the video *is* accomplishing something. It's not easy—"

Marina stopped at her locker. "That's for sure—"

"And I think they would like it, actually. I think they would be, I don't know, kind of . . . proud." My face grew a little warm when I said the last part.

"That's great," said Marina, twirling her locker combination. "Tell them that."

"But . . . I thought you were going to come up with a plan."

Marina shook her head. "I'm not so good with the plans these days. Really, just tell them what you told me." She pulled the books from her locker and snapped her lock shut.

"Okay," I said, "but if it doesn't go well, *I'm* coming to *your* house for dinner tonight."

Later that evening, I practically floated down the hall to my room. It felt like the air was humming as I clicked the door shut behind me.

Priyanka looked up from her desk. "What's wrong?"

"Nothing," I said. "Absolutely nothing. I asked Ma and Papa if it was okay for me to keep working on the video at lunch, and they said yes!"

"They did!" Priyanka put down her pencil. "I can't believe it. Why?"

I shook my head. "I don't know." I tried to replay the conversation, the thought of which had made me twirl my ring so much earlier that day, I'd nearly worn a groove in my thumb. "They just said that since it wasn't interfering with my schoolwork, and I'd come to them for permission, it was okay."

"Oh." Priyanka opened her container of pencil leads and poured them into her hand. "That's . . . I mean . . . that's good."

"What?" I went to sit on the bottom bunk. "I thought you'd be happy."

"I am. I just . . ." She put one lead on the desk and tried to slide the rest back into the container. "Maybe I should have asked to join chorus after all. I thought they'd say no because it goes until five . . ." One of the leads dropped, and she pressed her finger against the desk to pick it up.

"You can ask," I said. I didn't even know she liked to sing. "Maybe they're even in a good mood now. You know, from—"

"No." She slid the last lead in with the others. "You have to be in chorus from the beginning of the year."

"Oh." My heart squeezed a little. "That's too bad."

She shrugged and loaded up her pencil. "It's okay."

"I'm sure you can be in chorus in high school," I said. "Just think—no Test Prep, and a whole year before you have to start worrying about the SATs!"

"*If* I get into Stuyvesant," she said, trying out her new lead. "If I don't, I bet Ma and Papa will make me apply for tenth grade."

"Ugh." The thought made me shudder. Priyanka didn't seem bothered by the thought, though, and had already gone back to her homework. "Want me to quiz you on the vocab?" I asked. We both had quizzes in Test Prep the next day.

"When I'm done with my science," she said, circling something in her textbook. "That would be great."

I pulled my independent-reading book off the top bunk. "You know," I said, "Ma and Papa told me they wanted to see my video when I was done. I bet they would *really* like it if you let me interview you."

Priyanka snorted, but I could tell she liked that I'd asked again. "We'll see."

As I settled onto the bottom bunk with my book, I glanced down at my ring. The heavy gold lines twined around the onyx, making my fingers look longer, stronger. *Nani*, I thought, *thank you for giving me this ring, for calmness in the face of struggle, and for my family, who tries to make me into the person I want to be.*

MARINA'S LITTLE BLACK BOOK
Entry #21

* Best Idea: Sachi Parikh
You want to show the video in the lab?
You are a genius!
* Most Talented Directors: Marina Glass and
Sachi Parikh
Duh! Double duh!

"Wow," said Rachel, looking around the video lab, "I can't believe all these people are here."

"I know!" I was squealing like Addie, but I didn't care—all the chairs were taken! Not just with Elizabeth and our group, and Sachi's friends and her sister, but with Crystal, Natasha, and *Julian*, his feet up on the chair in front of him. He was laughing with Crystal and Natasha, and I thought, *Keep him in a good mood, ladies. I want him to think this video is the biggest woo in school.*

"Reener! Rachel!" Addie thumped the seats next to her. "Come sit!"

"Coming!" Rachel called. Then she hissed, "Marina?"

"What?"

"How's my hair?"

I looked at her half bun. "Fine."

"Good," she whispered back, "because I really think today is the day that Mr. Phillips is going to notice me."

I laughed as Rachel made her way to her seat. Then I mouthed to Addie, "I need to be up here." Sachi and I had to start the video, and Mr. Phillips wanted us to introduce ourselves—hotness! I was so glad Sachi had suggested that we ask to show our video in the video lab. This was way cooler than the Arts Assembly. It was an exclusive screening.

"All right, girls." Mr. Phillips came up to the front of the room, where Sachi and I were huddled in the corner. "Are you ready?"

I gulped. Sachi and I been working on our video for weeks now, and I had been excited to show it to people, but now they were actually going to see it! Then I remembered all the good things my mom had said about our video the week before, when she'd found me working on it. Even if her idea of hot fashion was pumpkin pants, it was cool to hear her say the video looked like it could be on TV.

I told Mr. Phillips, "We're ready."

"Good," said Mr. Phillips. "Go ahead." He nodded at the front of the room. I followed Sachi over there, my mouth suddenly dry.

"Hi, everyone," said Sachi, her hands clasped together. "Thanks for coming to our video"—she glanced at me, and I filled in the title—"*When It's Hot, When It's Not, and When It's Hot, Hot, Hot.*"

"Word!" called Julian, and my heart leapt. Everyone started clapping, even Mr. Phillips and—whoa! Ms. Avery was here! Sachi and I looked at each other as if to say, *Yikes! Here we go!*

"So," said Sachi, "I guess I'll press 'play' now."

Everybody laughed, and I smiled. Go, Sachi.

She bent down and started the video, and we hurried to the side of the room to watch.

Sachi and Marina's Video

NARRATOR'S VOICE (MARINA)
There are so many different trends
in this world.

VICTIM/VICTORIOUS footage: Rachel, Chelsea, Madison, Addie, Crystal, and Natasha on the red carpet. They strut. They laugh. They applaud themselves.

```
PAN: school lobby. T-shirts with tank tops
underneath. Hoodies, leggings, flats. Saggy
jeans, basketball sneakers.

     NARRATOR'S VOICE (SACHI)
     With all of those choices, how do
     people know—when it's hot, when
     it's not, and when it's hot, hot,
     hot?

CUT TO: interviews.

     INTERVIEWER (SACHI)
     So, how do you choose what to wear?

     TESSA
     I don't know. I guess I buy
     whatever's in the stores I like.

     INTERVIEWER (SACHI)
     How do you decide which stores to
     go to?

     TESSA
     Just . . . wherever my friends and
     I go . . . and I guess I just buy
     what looks good on me. And what my
     mom says I'm allowed to wear.
```

People laughed. I nudged Sachi and grinned. I remembered Mr. Phillips saying, "If they laugh in the first minute,
you've got 'em." Maybe we'd got 'em. Which was good,

because after the part with Sachi's friends, there was a part that made me nervous: *my* friends.

It had taken me almost a week after we'd made up to ask if I could interview them. When Sachi had asked, I'd put her off, saying, "I think we need to look at the title colors again." Eventually, though, she'd told me, "I think we're running out of things to edit. Do you think you can talk to your friends?"

I hadn't even told them I was doing another video; I'd just let them think I had detention during lunch. When I had made up with Elizabeth, I'd promised that I would never do anything else like *Victim/Victorious*, and I didn't want her to think I wasn't taking it seriously.

But finally, one afternoon at my house, I had told my friends about the new video and asked if I could interview them. At first Rachel had said "No thanks" and stuffed a Milano in her mouth.

"Please?" I asked. "You're, like, the only one of us who dresses different." I tried to ignore the bad luck of Milano the Cookie, who was being chomped to death between Rachel's jaws.

"I don't know," Rachel said around her mouthful. "I just keep thinking about what happened last time."

At the kitchen table, Elizabeth was gripping her Pepper bottle with both hands.

"Our video is nothing like last time," I said, "so don't worry. It's just—if you don't do it, Sachi's friends will be the only ones talking about how they know what's hot, and, I don't know. I think we should be in it too."

Rachel swallowed Mr. Milano. "Well, we don't want *those* girls to represent fashion."

"Right." I didn't exactly love her bad-mouthing Sachi's friends, but I wasn't going to mention that right now.

"Okay, fine." Rachel reached for the cookie bag and sighed. "Just let me know when, so I can bring on the hotness."

I knew I was going to laugh, so I grabbed my Pepper and gulped. Across the room Elizabeth was doing the same thing. Oh, thank God for Elizabeth. As long as one person knew that Rachel was a drama queen, I could sit through a thousand Milano stories.

Ooh—the part with my friends was coming up. I leaned in closer.

```
ADDIE
How do I know what looks good? Um,
I like the things at Abercrombie.


MADISON
Abercrombie.
```

```
CHELSEA
Abercrombie.

ADDIE
Oh, and Hollister.

MADISON
Hollister.

CHELSEA
I like Hollister.
```

Everybody laughed at that one. I couldn't believe it. When Sachi had said it would be funny to show everybody agreeing with each other, I'd said, "Why is that funny? Everybody knows what's cool." Hearing people laughing now, I realized it was weird that so many people thought the same thing. But wasn't that fashion? Wasn't that life?

Ooh . . . next up was the boys. This part was *definitely* funny.

```
INTERVIEWER (SACHI)
And how do you decide what to wear?

ALEX
If it's cold, I put on a sweater.
If it's hot, I put on a T-shirt. I
don't, like, think about it.
```

Rachel whispered to Elizabeth, "That's your boyfriend!"
Elizabeth sank low in her seat and Rachel grinned.

```
INTERVIEWER (MARINA)
How do you decide what to wear?

JULIAN
I like those guys selling
sweatshirts on 125th Street.

BOY'S VOICE (offscreen)
You buy your clothes on the street?

JULIAN
Shut up, man! It's cool!
```

Once again, everyone cracked up. Julian pumped his fists
in the air. Score! Conversation after the video, for sure. I didn't
even need to worry about fighting off Rachel, since she now
claimed to be in love with the guy playing the lead in the play.

```
NARRATOR (SACHI)
As you can see, a lot of people
look at what's going on around them
to tell them what's in style. But
some people get inspiration from a
different place: themselves.

PHOEBE
When I was in second grade, I
decided to wear an apron to school.
```

```
My mom and I had been cooking the
night before, and I had worn this
cute little orange apron with
pink flowers. I liked it so much
that I thought, This looks great.
I'm going to wear this to school
tomorrow over my jeans.

Then I got to school and my best
friend was like, "Why are you
wearing an apron?" And I was like,
"Um . . . I don't know!" It didn't
seem like such a good idea anymore,
so I put it in my locker.
```

That part always made me wonder: What was Phoebe's friend like now? Was she anything like me? Had she ever wanted to do what I had done to the person who was being interviewed next—Rachel?

```
RACHEL
People here just wear a tiny little
bit of what looks good. There are
a million different things to wear,
and I think, why not wear them?

CUT TO: Rachel leaning against a locker,
wearing a wrap dress and knee-high boots.

CUT TO: Rachel wearing pearl necklaces wound
around her wrists.
```

I looked at the real Rachel, who was holding out her arm and grinning, showing off the necklace bracelet I'd given her as a "thank you for being in my video" present. I still thought those things were butt-ugly, but it hadn't killed me to spend five dollars on something I knew she'd like. Her clothes didn't give me Parmesan mouth so much these days, anyway.

I had to admit I was kind of sick of thinking about clothes all the time. Eventually I wanted to make a video about something completely different. Would I write a script again? Stick with interviews? Who knew? Whatever it was, I knew I could make it hot, hot, hot.

Jessica Leader

SACHI'S ~~VIDEO NIGHTMARE~~ JUST PLAIN VIDEO #22.0

INTERIOR. THE VIDEO LAB—DAY

A fascinated audience sits in rows. Sachi
and Marina stand by a wall, watching in
excitement.

But Sachi's face clouds over.

They had liked it so far—a lot. Alex had pumped his fist
during his little interview, and Tessa's friends had all patted
her on the back when she'd said the thing about her apron.
But now we were coming to the part that had been the hard-
est for me to edit.

>   NARRATOR (SACHI)
>   What makes you decide to dress
>   differently from most people?
>
>   LAINEY
>   Halloween is my favorite holiday,
>   so why shouldn't every day be
>   Halloween? Wearing boring clothes
>   all the time is just . . . boring.

```
CUT TO: picture of Lainey, sitting back in a
chair, her pink Converse high-tops resting on
the seat in front of her, her legs covered in
stripy socks.

CUT TO: picture of girls waiting on line
for a movie, wearing Converse high-tops and
stripy socks.
```

Next to me Flora muttered something to Lainey.

"No," said Lainey, "I knew."

I'd been surprised when Marina told me that Lainey's look wasn't as original as I'd thought. "Sorry," she'd said. "But here, let me show you." She image-searched "girls wearing Converse sneakers" and instantly came with a whole page of pictures.

"Oh no," I said. "The whole point was that she was original. This just makes it look like she's copying people."

"Most people are copying somebody," Marina said. "Rachel definitely is."

"I guess." I stared at the screen full of girls who were dressed so much like Lainey, some of whom even had armfuls of bracelets. "Although—my sister and that koala bear key chain—no one has that."

"True," Marina agreed, closing the Google window. "She's on her own there."

When I thought of it that way, the koala bear was kind of cool.

"We should put that in the video, actually," Marina said, reopening the Internet. "People who think they're being original but really aren't."

"Really?" I looked at her uneasily. "I don't want to seem like I'm putting Lainey down."

"I'm not trying to slam her," Marina said, "but we shouldn't *not* include it. I mean, this is about how people know what's popular, right?"

Part of me had wanted to keep it a secret from Lainey, or to not invite her to the screening. But then I'd decided, no. I was anti-sneaking. I would tell her.

Lainey hadn't been surprised. "I never said I was the only person who dressed like that," she'd told me over the phone (I had gotten my phone privileges back!). "I'm just the only person at Jacobs who dresses that way, but all my friends from my old school have bicycle-chain necklaces."

```
NARRATOR (SACHI)
A lot of people are afraid to dress
differently because they think
people will make fun of them.
What would you tell them?
```

```
LAINEY
If you wear weird clothes, some
people will make fun of you. But
so what? You can't make everyone
happy, so you might as well make
yourself happy.

PHOEBE
You know, I kind of wish I'd told
my friend, "I like my apron! I'm
going to keep wearing my apron."
```

That was my favorite part. It was the reason I'd used my birthday money to buy a navy turtleneck sweater I'd seen on sale. Wearing it with one of the mirrored scarves my cousin had given me, I felt cool and grown-up, like the women on the DIRECT THIS poster. Okay, so maybe I was too excited about a piece of clothing, but everybody needed to wear something.

One or two people had given me odd looks the first time I'd worn the scarf, but Lainey had been right that if I decided not to care what people thought, I wouldn't mind as much. Priyanka had already known that. Speaking of . . . my heart started thudding as I realized what was coming next.

```
NARRATOR (MARINA)
One thing that's hard to understand
is why some trends get started in
the first place, and why they go
away.
```

CUT TO: Priyanka.

    PRIYANKA
    There are lots of reasons things
    become popular. Sometimes someone's
    trying to make money by deciding
    everyone needs to have this new
    thing. Sometimes a movie or TV show
    makes something cool, and sometimes
    . . . it's just a mystery. I mean,
    when I was little, I remember non-
    Indians wearing red bindi dots on
    their foreheads. Are they going to
    start selling saris at the Gap?
    Probably not, but you never know.

    You just decide how much you're
    going to care, and (shrugs) I don't
    know. (She pauses.) Are we done now?

People laughed. "Sachi!" Priyanka whispered.

"It's funny," I said. "Everybody likes it."

"Hmph," she said. But I could tell she was pleased.

CUT TO: the studio (Ms. Avery's homeroom),
with Sachi and Marina sitting behind two
desks.

    MARINA
    And now our show draws to a close.

SACHI
As you have seen, there are many
ways to decide what is hot.

MARINA
You can follow trends.

SACHI
Shop with your friends!

MARINA
You can do your own thing.

SACHI
Don't worry about what people
think!

MARINA
There's no one way to do it—

SACHI
—so do what you want to do and have
fun.

CUT TO: Madison and Chelsea, showing off
identical sweaters; Rachel's red cowboy
boots; Lainey's pink sneakers; Priyanka's
koala bear key chain.

ROLL CREDITS.

"Woo-hoo!"

"Encore!"

Then people started chanting, "Ma-ree-na! Ma-ree-na!" and "Sa-chi! Sa-chi!"

I whispered, "I'll get the lights."

My friends rushed over to me. "That was so cool!" exclaimed Lainey. "I never realized that, the way stores try to make you buy things. Now I'm going to—well, I don't know what. I have to think about it."

Priyanka and I exchanged smiles.

"Sachi," said Flora admiringly, "nice job."

"Eee!" Phoebe threw her arms around me. "You talked about my apron! I love my apron!"

I laughed and felt myself blush. No one ever fussed over me like this, except in the Ahmedabad airport.

"Hey, Sachi," said a scratchy voice.

I turned and saw—Alex! I had been so excited when I'd seen him in the crowd, but I wasn't sure if I'd have the nerve to talk to him.

"Hey," he said, "that was good."

"Thanks!" His green elastics were *so* cute. "You did a good job too. I mean, I liked your interview."

He grinned. "Thanks. See you later."

"Bye."

He stepped away from me and my friends and called, "Bye, Elizabeth!"

"What? Oh, bye!" called Elizabeth from across the room.

I watched him leave—Alex with his cute, loping stride—and then realized Flora and Lainey were staring at me.

"What?" I asked.

They burst out laughing.

"You so like him!" said Flora.

"Shh!" I said, glancing at Elizabeth to make sure she wasn't looking.

"But you do, right?" Flora whispered.

I bit my lip, squinched my eyes shut, and nodded.

"Aw," said Flora. "Yeah, he is kind of cute . . . even if he is a royal pain."

"You guys." Priyanka tapped her watch. "The bell is going to ring soon."

"Yikes!" said Lainey. As soon as my friends started picking up their backpacks, Marina's friends did too. They all gave me one last congrats and left.

It was then that I realized, oh, disaster! We'd totally rearranged the room, and we had to put it back for Mr. Phillips's class that afternoon. I was about to start dragging chairs when Ms. Avery approached me.

"I'm so glad you invited me," she said, smiling. "That was wonderful." She gave me a hug, and then, to my complete surprise, she gave Marina one too. Marina looked shocked at first, but from the way she looked at the floor, biting her lip even as she smiled, I thought she might have appreciated it.

Mr. Phillips came over, holding out the DVD for me to take. "You girls did a great job," he said. "I can't believe all that cutting you did—from one scene to the next to the next. Most people don't have the patience. Did that take a long time?"

"*Yes.*" Marina said it like a groan, and we all laughed.

"Thanks for letting us use your room," I told Ms. Avery. "We never could have done all that without your computers."

"Yeah, thanks," Marina added. "And Mr. Phillips, thanks for, um, you know, letting us show the video up here. Even if we're not in the real class."

He nodded. "It was my pleasure."

Ms. Avery smoothed her curls. "I'm going to miss having you girls up during lunch. I've kind of gotten used to it."

"I'm going to miss the melba toast," Marina put in. "That stuff is addictive."

Once Ms. Avery left, Marina and I began moving the chairs back into place. My arms started to ache, and strangely, the rest of me ached too. I joined Marina at the back of the lab, where we had stashed our backpacks.

"Hey," she said, "we did it!"

"I know!" I cried. "We did!"

We slapped each other five, then gave each other a hug.

"So," she said, letting go, "you have English. But you probably brought your books."

"Right," I said, smiling. "Do you have your books for science?"

"No. Stop at my locker?"

We thanked Mr. Phillips one last time and I grabbed my things, my Jabber Monkeys pencil case sitting on top of my books. I had stopped shielding it from Marina a while back.

Once we got to her locker, Marina tucked her hair behind her ear and said, "Well…"

"Yeah. See you—" I broke off. For the past few weeks, if we passed each other in the halls, we'd say, "See you at lunch." But we wouldn't see each other at lunch the next day. We'd sit in the same lunchroom, but with different people, probably talking about totally different things. "Just—see ya," I said.

She smiled. "See ya," she replied, and dialed her combination.

SACHI'S VIDEO NIGHTMARE FANTASY #22.1

INTERIOR. SECOND-FLOOR HALLWAY—DAY

I walked toward English, laughing at myself. We'd been so caught up in making our video that some days, everything I did seemed like a screenplay.

```
Sachi walks into English class, where
everyone bursts into applause.
```

No. My applause was done. But then, so were the nightmares. Priyanka hadn't exposed my secret. Mr. Phillips hadn't laughed in my face. Marina hadn't destroyed me. But I'd spent so much time worrying that the nightmares would come true, I'd made things worse. I'd made extra nightmares come true.

No more video nightmares, I decided. Just videos.

SACHI'S LIFE: A VIDEO JUST FOR FUN #22.2

```
Sachi walks down the empty hallway, a spring
in her step.

CLOSE-UP on her armful of books and Jabber
Monkeys pencil case. Light bounces off her
onyx ring.

FADE TO BLACK.
```

About the Author

Jessica Leader grew up in New York City. Like Marina and Sachi, she had many important conversations in the stairwells of her school and on the cross-town bus. In addition to being a writer, she has taught English and drama in New York and Louisville, Kentucky. Jessica graduated from Brown University and has an MFA in writing for children and young adults from the Vermont College of Fine Arts. *Nice and Mean* is her first novel. It is all fiction, except for the part about wearing an apron to school. For more about the story of the apron, as well as her thoughts about books and what she's writing now, visit her website at www.jessicaleader.com.